Praise for King

"A tight, fast-paced thriller with intense action and sharp dialogue, *Lethal Liaisons* is layered with justice, dark human truths, and a protagonist you can't help but root for—this is a Jack West novel you won't forget."
~ **Foram Vyas for Readers' Favorite**

ISBN: 979-8-9856982-8-2

Edited by

Book Cover by Chandra Fry @ stainedglasspublix.wixsite.com/ppromo
ting

Published by: Deanna King Writing

deannakingwriting.com

A Pile of Gray Bones

Deanna King

Deanna King Writing

Dedication

To Dad
Had you not moved us around a lot I would have never
experienced the life of rural town America.

Prologue

CHARLIE BRAKED, TURNED ON his blinker, and sighed.

Traffic wasn't too congested. Not yet.

He'd arrived an hour early. The parking lot reflected it—plenty of empty spaces. He parked near the front and sat for a moment, scanning the town.

Sidewalks. Storefronts. Three- and five-story office buildings. A twenty-four-hour mini emergency room sat dark. A hair salon shared space with a barber shop. Several nail shops lined the street, all closed at this hour. The dry cleaners, however, were already open and ready for business.

The expanded post office, the UPS Store, and the new automated car wash next door were still asleep—but not for long. Alice's Sewing Room sat beside Holly's Tea Room, both catering to the same steady group of women who'd been coming for years.

At the far corner stood Ted's Burgers—an oddly named hamburger joint that had somehow survived—along with a Taco Bell and a Golden Chick. At the other end of town were McDonald's, Jack in the Box, and Long John Silver's. Down a few side streets, you might stumble upon a Mexican restaurant, a Sonic, or a sports bar already advertising beer and wings.

Charlie locked his door. A habit now. One he'd picked up over the years, though it still felt strange.

Mom-and-Pop's Café sat near the edge of the lot. The automated opener hummed and swooshed the door open as he approached. Cool air washed over his face before the door sealed shut behind him.

He chose a table by the window.

When the server came by, he asked for a carafe of coffee and creamer and told her he was expecting friends to join him in about an hour.

By his third cup, Charlie found himself staring through the large, double-paned picture window. The glass needed washing—on the outside. It hadn't rained in weeks. No excuse for it to be that dirty.

Not that the view was worth the effort.

Brick-and-mortar buildings. Blacktop roads. Sidewalks. Stoplights. Traffic beginning to thicken.

The air carried the smell of tar, gasoline, exhaust, and dust. Engines revved. Cars sputtered and backfired. Construction crews worked nearby, patching potholes and widening roads to accommodate the steady influx of people moving into the area.

Streetlights and oversized business signs burned day and night. New billboards appeared constantly—advertising businesses, lawyers, or subdivisions *coming soon*. Ten miles south, a new high-school football stadium was rising from the dirt, scheduled to be ready by the fall after next.

Deeper in the city, new elementary schools seemed to appear overnight. School boundaries shifted. Neighborhoods were redrawn.

From the roof of a three-story office building a quarter mile from the café, anyone standing there would see an ocean of rooftops. Fenced yards. Identical swing sets. Pools, hot tubs, and manicured gardens—all governed by homeowners' associations.

Gone were the days of making your own decisions about the home you bought with your hard-earned money. You needed permission to plant a tree. To add shrubs. To choose certain flowers. Wait too long to mow or skip the edging, and you got a warning.

Charlie smiled.

He would never have that problem. He wasn't a sell-out. He'd stood his ground and let progress surround him over the years, but not beat him down or take control of his life or his lifestyle.

His phone chirped.

It was Evan. *Running a few minutes behind. Stopping for gas.*

Charlie sent a thumbs-up emoji—something he'd never imagined doing back when he was a teenager, or even knowing the word *emoji.*

Another message came in. *BTW, Bruce is riding with me.*

Charlie replied with the OK symbol.

The café door swooshed open, and Neal sauntered in. He pulled out a chair, waved at the server, and said, "Another coffee cup, please." Then he turned to Charlie, grinning, and stuck out his hand. "Charlie. How're you doing?"

"Good. Doing good." Charlie shook his hand. "You on a big job? Haven't seen you in a few months."

Neal Swanson had left for vocational school during their senior year to become an electrician. He'd completed his apprenticeship, earned his journeyman status, and eventually passed the test to reach master level. He stayed in the Austin–San Antonio area for years before coming home to marry Holly Randolph. Eight years ago, they moved back, and Holly opened the Tea Room. Neal never sold his family land. Instead, they rebuilt the old homestead from the ground up.

Bruce had spent his life in the oilfields, traveling wherever the work took him. Offshore or land—it didn't matter. After more than twenty-one years, he'd finally decided it was a young man's job.

Evan Dyer's plans shifted over time but always kept him in law enforcement and rooted in Station County, which pleased his wife, Audra. He planned to run for sheriff again in the next election—unopposed. He was that kind of guy.

Charlie had chosen ranch life and carried it on after his pop passed. He missed his father. His mother, Lindy, had always been the backbone of the family, but she was slowing now, showing signs of dementia that worried him and his sister, Libby.

Gregg's Army career gave him the chance to pursue medicine—animal medicine. He took courses online while serving, added extras when he could, and later used his GI Bill to attend Texas A&M. Veterinary school followed, along with years of hard work. Koller Veterinary was proof that determination paid off.

Charlie had never been prouder of his big brother.

Libby graduated from Texas Tech shortly after old man Adair passed away. With no children of his own, Adair left parcels of land to the four boys and Libby. The largest went to her. Charlie bought it at a fair price, expanding the Koller Ranch. Neal, Evan, and Bruce sold their portions to a newcomer raising goats.

Libby married Keith Polston and moved to Twisted Pine Ranch near Hunt, Texas—far from town, far from progress. She called newcomers *carpetbaggers*. Charlie suspected she'd watched *Gone With the Wind* one too many times.

She was the real thing—a modern-day cattlewoman. Charlie had once looked it up out of curiosity. Margaret Heffernan Borland. The comparison fit.

Mobile phones. Internet. Email. Google. Streaming. Social media. Amazon. None of it existed when they were kids—not until their teens. And once it started, it never slowed.

When they were twelve, they wished to be thirteen. Then sixteen. Then eighteen. Then twenty-one.

Time crawled. Then jogged.

Then it ran.

Nothing slowed it down.

The passage of time.

He squeezed his eyes shut. In a blur, the years bunched together like a colorful cinematic reel with Dolby sound. Exhaling deeply, he relaxed his face, his eyes still closed as his mind hit rewind—carrying him from this day back to a simpler time. A time before progress closed in on them, and before death touched any of their lives.

1

PLACES LIKE THIS USED to be out in the country. People moved here to get away from it all—away from the noise, the crowds, the constant rush.

Too bad it all caught up with them anyway.

Houses once sat acres apart, fenced off for livestock and privacy. They were set back on the land, dirt roads leading to wide front porches. The homes had every creature comfort—just none of the city noise bleeding in after dark.

Nights used to belong to the stars. Trillions of them. Bright enough to swallow the darkness. Before streetlights, shopping centers, and parking lots dimmed the sky into something smaller.

Sheds and hay barns stood a hundred yards behind the houses. Fenced pens held troughs and rolled bales of hay. Tractors rested where they were left. Minibikes lay on their sides. Kids ran free. Dogs did what dogs were meant to do. Barn cats hunted field mice and slept full in the hay.

No one worried about traffic. There was room to breathe.

Fire pits glowed in the evenings. Old lawn chairs creaked. The smell of manure and hay drifted on the breeze, familiar and comforting.

This was where people came when they wanted refuge—when they wanted land they refused to sell, no matter the offer. Ranchers. Farmers. Folks who owned cattle, horses, donkeys. Sometimes a llama. Once in a while, even a zebra.

They worked the land because it was who they were.

Then the developers came.

Road crews. Contractors. New highways. Strip centers. Chain stores. Gas stations. Restaurants stacked between parking lots. Lights that burned all night and erased the stars.

People arrived in waves—city folks in a hurry, chasing convenience and zero-lot lines. They came from everywhere, all at once, like an invasion.

Before them, life had been simple.

And calm.

2

1984

They'd had to make the eighty-mile round trip into town to buy lumber to repair the barn and barbed wire to replace fencing on the back four acres.

Gregg hadn't wanted to go, so Charlie and Dad made it a father-and-youngest-son outing.

On a brisk fall Saturday morning, they drove along the old highway with the windows rolled down. Crisp air carried the scent of freshly mowed grass and hay.

At the five-mile mark off County Road 1821, Charlie waved at Bruce Rafferty's house. At ten miles, he waved at Evan Dyer's. In the opposite direction, Neal Swanson lived just past the nine-mile mark.

They were his best friends, all living within a five- to ten-mile radius.

The aged truck bounced along dirt roads before reaching the asphalt highway that led into town. Dad's pickup kicked up white dust and gravel as it passed harvested fields of hay, corn, wheat, and cotton.

John Deere combines and tractors dotted the empty land.

After several twists and turns, Paul Koller's blue-and-white '73 Ford F-150 slowed at the end of the gravel road and turned onto the first paved stretch leading toward town. The ride smoothed out once the tires hit asphalt. Charlie and his dad rested their forearms on the window frames, letting the wind roll in.

Neither of them spoke. They simply enjoyed being.

Charlie watched the landscape glide by, the colors of fall rich and unspoiled. Deep down, he knew he was—and always would be—a country boy.

Paul stopped at a four-way intersection and turned onto the main road. Fifteen miles later, they reached the roadwork Texas DOT had started more than a year earlier.

The road was torn up, widened to prepare for heavier traffic. Developers had bought large tracts of land outside the city limits of Dove Crossing, clearing the way for housing developments.

"This old country road will be a six-lane highway before long," Paul said, his voice heavy.

Charlie studied the piles of dirt, gravel, and sand. Excavators and bulldozers sat scattered across the land.

"Yep. They've cleared a lot already," he said, pointing. "Look at those piles."

Heaps of uprooted shrubs and brush sat stacked where wooded land once stood. Some of them looked like they'd make a hell of a bonfire.

Dead brush lay beneath fallen trees—rained on, snowed on, infested with bugs and rats. Charlie was sure snakes tunneled underneath, hibernating and laying eggs.

The mounds had never interested him before. Until today.

"Hey, Dad?"

"Yeah?"

"Why do they leave those piles sitting there?"

Paul glanced over. "The brush?"

"Yeah. Old man Adair's got some like that too, only nobody sees his. These are right out here on the road. Kinda ugly. Why don't they mulch it or turn it into compost? Don't snakes and rats hide in it?"

"You've got some good points, Charlie Boy," Paul said, giving him a brief smile. "Sometimes they're used as windbreaks. Other animals burrow underneath to stay warm. Sometimes they leave it to decompose. Other times they haul it off if they're building."

"Guess that makes sense," Charlie said. "Still looks weird."

Paul frowned slightly. "Weird how?"

Charlie studied the heaps again. "Not brush. To me, it looks like a pile of gray bones."

Paul shrugged. "Everyone sees things differently, I suppose."

IN TOWN, THEY STOPPED at the local lumberyard and hardware store. Lumber filled the truck bed. Dad bought a new gas-powered chainsaw, along with nails, a hammer, and a handsaw.

They picked up seed packets and fertilizer Mom had asked for. She planted carrots, beets—Charlie hated beets—onions, snap peas, and bush beans.

His ten-year-old sister, Libby, loved helping Mom in the garden. She loved animals and didn't mind getting dirty. Most girls in his school were tomboys; country life bred that kind of kid.

Charlie figured Libby reminded him of their old neighbor, Gus Adair.

Mr. Adair was a confirmed bachelor who kept to himself, though he got along well with the boys. They rode his donkeys across his land. He raised pygmy goats and grew collard greens, poke salad, corn, and more tomato plants than Charlie could count.

The boys ate tomatoes straight off the vine. The corn, Adair claimed, was for his jackasses—a joke that never failed to make them laugh.

A couple of years earlier, Adair had cleared part of his back acreage, leaving several gray piles behind.

"Building a barn?" Charlie had asked.

"Nope. I'll buy a wood chipper next spring, add goat manure, and make my own fertilizer," the old man said. "Anything I don't use, I let decompose."

That answer had satisfied Charlie. At least those piles would serve a purpose.

———

CHARLIE'S GRANDPA, ANGUS KOLLER, had built the ranch and left its two hundred fifteen acres to his only son, Paul. They raised cattle and kept a few horses. Mom raised chickens and sold eggs. She had a green thumb and managed two large garden plots.

Five hundred yards behind the barn stood the chicken coops and her gardening shed. Behind that was a storage shed for feed and her small tractor—the baby version of Dad's John Deere.

The old farmhouse sat three-quarters of a mile off the county road. On bad-weather days, Mom drove the kids to catch the school bus.

Behind the house and barn stretched five open acres—space to roam, camp under the stars, fly kites, and let imagination run free.

The land held hand-dug stock tanks and natural fishing ponds. The one closest to the house had a tire swing hanging from a large tree.

Pure summer entertainment.

It was a good life for a growing boy—though chores came with it. Barns needed sweeping. Hay needed hauling. Gardens needed weeding twice a week.

Friends lived miles away. The school bus gathered them from across the countryside and carried them off together.

For now, this community remained untouched by developers.

A clean, wholesome life.

But for how long?

Sometimes, the future wasn't always something to look forward to.

3

School ended forty days ago, and summer was in full swing.

Minibikes brought your friends to visit; who needed a driver's license on a country road, right?

Eleven- or twelve-year-old boys who were curious and innocent.

Kids who were not exposed to things like drugs, malicious behavior, or guns used for shady reasons.

Out here, they only used their guns for hunting dove, quail, and the occasional rabbit or fox who dug in Mom's garden.

None had a mind to be evil; they were having way too much fun being ... boys.

This year, out on the back five acres, thick with trees and brush, the boys were planning to build a tree-house.

After the old barn had a makeover, there was extra lumber. Charlie asked Dad if he and his friends could construct a treehouse.

Dad said, "Heck yes, Charlie, why not? Only you four gotta be careful out there and pick a solid tree, like the one at the back east corner. Don't go up too high. I still have the load wagon hooked up to my tractor, and I'll haul the lumber for you boys."

Charlie, jumping up and down, full of a boy's energy, tugged at his dad's shirttail.

"Lemme drive the truck, will ya? I can carry hammers, saws, nails. Will ya, huh? Will ya?"

It wasn't the first time Charlie had driven his old truck, and who'd care? It was his land, his kid, and his truck. Charlie's dad was the best.

Mom, well, she'd say yes too, but would be in the truck, in the driver's seat, letting him steer, and that wasn't driving—it was steering.

"Ask your mom to make some sandwiches and take a cooler of water and some old plastic cups, and stop to rest when you get tired, and Charlie, you boys wear your hats. Don't want you getting sunstroke."

"Hey, Dad?"

"Hmm?"

"If we get too hot, is it okay if I take the truck to the tank so we can swim after?"

Paul stood still, thinking about it. Back when he was a kid ... lots he did... stuff he shouldn't have; only he never asked permission. Charlie was a terrific kid, and he trusted him.

"Only out to the tank, no further," he checked his watch, "and be home by dinner, around five. We clear?"

"Yes, sir. I'll go ask Mom for the sandwiches, chips, and water." The boy took a step, and his father's voice stopped him. "Oh, don't tell her about the truck, you know Mom."

Charlie's eyes widened. "I sure do. Come on, Bruce, let's go call and see if Evan and Neal are on the way, and I'll ask Mom about the food."

SWEAT AND DIRT COVERED each boy's young, tanned face as they hammered, sawed, and constructed a tree-house.

Charlie's pop had stayed and helped get the floor constructed and hauled up to the middle limb and mounted, so he felt comfortable with the boys standing that high up.

"Lord, son, if you fell..." Paul looked at each boy. "Any of you breaking a leg, arm, or your neck, Mom would kill me."

"Thanks, Dad, this is super. Now we got it from here." Charlie's dark boy brows arched.

"Yeah, okay, I'm leaving, but hey, don't nail yourself to the wood planks, and for God's sake, be careful and don't fall off. You boys spot each other, hear me?"

"Loud and clear, Mr. Koller," Evan, Bruce, and Neal called out, and Charlie said, "Yes, Dad."

Paul Koller left the four boys, their laughter and roughhousing fading behind him, and he sighed. Oh, how he yearned for those boyhood days again.

On the tractor, he turned back toward the farm-house, the old John Deere rumbling over the land, cracking branches, snapping twigs, leaving tire-track imprints in the dirt.

"You got a pretty cool dad, Charlie," Evan said as he took a handful of nails and dumped them into his pocket.

"Yeah, wish my dad would let me drive his truck."

"My word, Neal, your dad has a Dually. That's too much truck for you, dude. I mean, you're only twelve."

"And a half," Neal blurted in defense.

"You got a minibike, be happy," Bruce said, "and Evan, you have a killer three-wheeler, so y'all shut up."

"You shut up, Bruce. You're the only one of us that has a camel."

It was true; Bruce's dad had bought a camel from a carny man who was getting out of the business.

Poor camel, headed to the glue factory or wherever camels get euthanized, and when Oren Rafferty found out that the man was going to put the camel down, the big man's heart broke.

The camel was young, fifteen years old, and he learned they could live to be forty or fifty. It was like they were cutting the poor animal down in its prime.

The big joke was when Oren let Bruce give the new addition to the family a name.

"Let's call him Smokey."

"Why not name him, like, Ali Baba or some Egyptian name?" his sister Audra asked.

"Nah, it's just that he looks like that camel on that cigarette package, the one called 'Camels,' so it fits him better."

They laughed so hard, Bruce's parents almost peed themselves.

———————

"How about we stop and rest a minute? Besides, I gotta go pee, and I'm getting hungry."

"Me too. I mean, I'm hungry," Evan said as he climbed down the ladder made of scrap wood, nailed to the trunk of the gigantic tree.

PB and J sandwiches, bags of either Cheetos or Fritos, and ice water from the water cooler Charlie's mom had loaded full of ice and water.

They discussed the plans for the house, or what sounded better to them was 'fort.'

"Hey, when we get her built and ready, let's ask our parents if we can camp out here one night. We can see if Charlie's dad will come out with us and help build a fire, and we can do weenies and chips and roast marshmallows."

"Yeah, maybe he will," Charlie said, with a mouth full of peanut butter and jelly sandwich. "If he doesn't, then maybe my big brother can come out here with us."

"Gregg?" Bruce eyed them all. "Not sure that would be very fun."

"Oh, come on, Bruce, Gregg ain't that bad. He's better than having a prissy big sister, like Audra."

"Your sister's nice, Bruce," Evan garbled with his mouth full of Fritos.

Bruce rolled his eyes. "Uh-huh, it's only because you gotta crush on her, Evan. That's why you assume she's nice. Only you don't hafta live with her— I do."

Neal spoke up. "Heard she has a crush on that new boy, the one that lives in the giant house. You know, down past old man Adair's place,"

Charlie washed down the last bit of his sandwich with a drink, then wiped his mouth with the back of his hand. "My brother doesn't like the guy, says he's, uh, whatchamacallit, conceited, or that other word, I can't remember how to say."

"Yeah, he's a narcissist. Means he's in love with himself," Evan stated.

"Yep, that's what Gregg says. He also said the guy's a real douchebag at school because he's got money. Oh, and my brother says he's got a mean streak in him."

"Hate to break it to ya, Charlie, but Gregg can be mean, too." Bruce sat back, a frown on his face.

"Aw, Bruce, one time he gives you a hard wedgie, and you gotta hold that against him forever. My brother's okay." Charlie took up for Gregg.

"Uh-huh, it wasn't your underwear he ripped when he yanked them so far up that, well, I thought my boys were gonna pop off." Bruce covered his privates when he spoke.

Neal jumped in. "Your boys? What, those shriveled-up grapes?"

Silence ... then peals of laughter.

"Come on, fellas, let's get the sides done, then go skinny-dipping in the tank." Charlie got them back to work.

Four boys, best buds; sawed, hammered, and nailed, and the planned treehouse/fort began taking a shape all its own. It was, as they stood back and surveyed their work two hours later, a masterpiece.

With his hands at his hips, Charlie said, "Help me load the tools up in the truck and stack the lumber, then we can come back tomorrow and start earlier while it's cooler. Let's go swimming."

Working gear squared away, lumber sitting in mismatched heaps, the four piled into the front seat of the old truck, and Charlie put it in gear, and they took off down the grassy dirt road headed to the stock tank.

The tank worked as their swimming hole all summer.

Bruce, Neal, and Evan had swimming holes on their property, too, but what made it more fun at the Koller stock tank was the large tree and the tire swing.

The boys flung themselves all afternoon, trying to outdo each other at who could go the highest.

4

At the crest of a hill, twelve miles away, a teenage boy sat atop a horse, field glasses on his nose, scanning the area.

His gaze landed on the stock tank where four boys swam. He watched, his expression that of impassive coldness.

He moved the glasses over the area, narrowing his eyes.

Old man Adair was puttering around in his stupid garden, wearing that ridiculous, wide-brimmed straw hat. He wore his grungy faded old-man overalls, his pant legs tucked into his worn-out work boots.

Cold eyes moved his sights to the old barn and those dumb goats who bleated, screamed, and dropped goat dung all day long.

And don't get him started on the old codger's four donkeys. The horrid braying added to the bleating; the sounds carried in the wind, and at feeding time, all he dreamed about was getting his shotgun and shooting them all, shutting them up forever; then shooting the old man, too.

He slipped the glasses back into the case and then shoved that into the old pannier he had attached to his saddle.

A swift kick in the flanks and his gelding jumped into motion, and he pulled the reins to the right to turn back. At a steady gallop, he moved towards the rear of his parents' one-hundred- thirty-acre parcel of land.

They'd cleared fifteen acres up front to build a house far larger than they needed, and it appeared to the town and outskirt residents that his parents were flaunting their wealth. A mark against him before he started his life in a new place.

His father had dreams of being a rancher, which was pure foolishness. Pop was all show; he had no idea about ranching; and besides, he already had money, plenty of it, so he did not need to raise cattle to make a living.

And, Lord, his mother was the ultimate snob of snobs. Her fancy country house where she acted all high and mighty. Another strike against him once the ladies of Hotspur had to deal with her.

He hated his parents for bringing them to this stupid wilderness. A place for hicks, hayseeds, and clodhoppers … all terms meaning ignorant hillbillies. Doug Lewison hated Texas; his roots were in The Bay Area; he was and always would be a Californian.

Off his mount, he pulled the reins and walked to a clump of trees that created a mini windbreak. He picked a shady spot to tie up his horse so he could sit and ruminate.

He pulled a flask out of the left pannier and a journal bound with thick rubber bands. His back against the larger of the trees, he sat, uncapped the flask, and took a long pull. Jim Beam. Dear old dad never once missed any bottles he'd snatched.

It amused him.

His father confided in him that his mother was a closeted whiskey drinker; but never got drunk.

Ha!

One thing he saw was his dear old mom never drank whiskey; she was a 'martini' gal. His father was old and clueless.

His parents.

One day they'd kick the bucket. This was a nice thought and he mumbled, "Or maybe I can help them cross over, sooner than later." Oh, if only.

After removing the rubber bands, he let the journal fall open to a random spot and smiled. Yeah- this was the perfect one to relive.

With a reverent touch, he lifted the photo, and he stared into the eyes of the lifeless body of a young drug addict.

He'd gotten more skilled with animals by the time he had gotten to her.

Animals had been okay to practice on; but damn it, people missed their dumb pets to the point of calling out the National Guard. To keep crap from spiraling out of control, he began scouring the dirty parts of the Bay Area, his main target area, San Francisco.

He sighed; he sure missed surfing, too.

His gaze moved back to the Kodak Polaroid, worn and fading.

The tiny girl in her early twenties; a crackhead, and not ugly yet because the drugs hadn't ruined her but were on the verge of doing so.

The violent death, the act itself ... an exhilarating rush. Better than any animal he'd done; and it was his first; just before his fifteenth birthday.

And it'd been easy to dispose of her body since he'd found her down by the docks, pimping herself out to dock workers, trying to earn cash for her next fix.

After dumping her into the bay, he watched her float off. As luck would have it, her clothes caught on a piece of ragged metal on the tanker's side keel scheduled to sail to Shanghai. After the tanker docked, maintenance crew found bits of the dead girl's clothes and her body, anything that hadn't gotten devoured by ocean life.

Law officials did all they could to piece it together but concluded that she'd been a druggy who fell in the San Francisco Bay and drowned.

He'd gotten away with his first murder, and he was only fourteen.

LONELINESS WASHED OVER HIM.

An only child with parents who had never expected to bear children. He'd become the light of their miserable rich lives; they coddled him, they fretted, and they placated him.

Doug got whatever he wanted whenever he asked. Neither of his parents, comfortable in showing affection nor had any parental warmth. What they knew were dollar signs.

They bought their love. A life growing up without siblings, just adults; nannies, servants; and their old friends; heavy emphasis on old- aged-spotted, wrinkled friends.

Texas.

No surf: no large waterways where he was, out in Podunk Hicksville.

Excitement is what he needed.

He'd seen a flyer on the wall at the town grocer's where the residents were planning a summer festival; food, fun, with music and a DJ, to host a dance to end the night. It wasn't a rock concert or close; but better than sitting at home twiddling his darned thumbs.

He hadn't had a girl back in Cali; but he'd had his eyes on a few. Some chicks he wanted to kiss and be nice too, the others he preferred to rumble with in the back seat; there were plenty of those types at his old school.

Country girls were different; or so he imagined.

There weren't many girls to choose from. A few of them were okay-looking. Some of them were bigger gals, with big boobs and muscles, country chicks who worked like farmhands.

Most of these girls weren't pretty, just average, and could whoop his butt. Maybe he could talk one of them into taking a wild ride in the back seat of his parents' fancy Lincoln.

Oh, how he longed for something to satisfy his growing appetite. Those naked boys: something he'd never considered back in Cali. Out here in no-man's land, there's not a lot to be choosy with.

Doug twisted the rubber bands around his journal, then took another swig from the flask.

Time to get back to the pretentious mansion he hated and to the old farts who might call the Sheriff out to find him.

Damned worry warts.

ON THE BANK, LYING sprawled out, four boys pondered girls, why they always went around in groups, and why they giggled so much?

"Your parents taking you to the festival?" Evan propped up on his side to look at his friends.

"Mine are, they gotta go since they're on some committee thingy," Bruce said.

"Yep. My mom's supervising the foodstuff, so I'm going too," said Neal. "And my sister Tara and her friends are decorating the civic center for the dance."

Charlie was quiet, and Bruce nudged him. "Hey, you are going, or what?"

"Yeah, and I was just thinking about the dance. You guys going to ask any girls to dance?"

Silence. For a moment, they were all silent, each lost in the thoughts of girls.

"Evan, you plan on asking Audra to dance?" Neal spurred him on.

"Shut up, and yeah, I just might." His brows dipped, and he turned to Bruce. "You figure your sister would dance with me?"

A snarl wrinkled Bruce's nose when he said, "Audra's fourteen and you're almost twelve. What do you think she'll say? I'm going with nope and telling you that you might as well ask Kadie Hopkins."

"The prom queen?" Evan wondered what the heck Bruce was talking about.

"You think Kadie Hopkins would dance with me?" Neal's heart thudded at the thought.

Charlie watched, not interjecting a word, waiting for Bruce to put the hammer down on Neal's hopes.

"Nah, but it'd be hilarious to watch you try to get her to dance with you, shoot we'd all buy tickets, right, guys?"

"Bruce Rafferty you're a butthole, you know that?" Neal tossed the wadded-up weeds he had been fiddling with at Bruce's head and missed.

"I'm asking Lyssa to dance," Charlie said, stunning the others into silence.

Lyssa: the prettiest girl in the entire sixth, seventh, and eighth grades. Also, the shyest and the smartest.

"Well dang it, Charlie Koller, we didn't know. When did you get a thing for Lyssa?" Neal asked.

"Same day as you three bozos did, I guess, the day she walked in as the new girl."

Charles Jason Koller had noticed Lyssa Caldwell, with a thudding heart and sweating palms.

On her first day, every boy in junior high had walked by the office to see who the new girl was. In a small rural area, if a new kid showed up it was big news.

Even that snotty rich boy that no one took to. This had been exciting news, and the older girls were eager to meet him. A novelty for a few months, but it wore off in a hurry once his true personality presented itself.

Doug Lewison, a native of California, looked down his nose at the country bumpkins and the way of life they enjoyed.

He knew what they whispered behind their hands as he walked through the halls of the old, musty school building. He didn't have any interest in sports or joining Four -H and acted more remorse than happy most days.

Charlie heard the girls say he had what they called a sad, brooding handsomeness.

They later labeled him a menacing rich brat.

Some girls continued to find him cute. Each had a secret wish that she could be the one to win him over to the simple joys of country living, curing him of his homesickness for California.

———

"IF HE'D GET HIS head outta his ass and just be a nice guy and laugh, maybe tryout for baseball or whatever, he could fit in, but he ain't even trying, mom."

"Well, Gregg, why don't you make friends with him, see if you can make him feel more at home." Charlie overheard Mom telling his older brother.

"Yeah, I was all set to see if he wanted to go fishing with us, but the turd head shoved me out of his way, and against the lockers, called me a hayseed, and told me to watch the hell where I was walking. Mom," Gregg shrugged with that kind of 'do I hafta' look on his face.

Noticing his mom's expression, her half-smile with her subtle head shake, Charlie heard Lindy Koller say, "I'm sure he's just very homesick, Gregg, and that's making him sad and angry."

"Well, until he gets a better attitude and, over his homesickness, he won't have any friends here in Hotspur."

5

HOTSPUR, TEXAS. THE TOWN'S population, about 411, fluc-
tuated with births, deaths, and new families moving in. "Town" was generous — a few buildings and
two stoplights. Most streets inside the city limits were
paved, except for a few side roads leading to small res-
idential areas. There were factory-built homes scattered across the region, single- and double-wide trailers mixed in with older houses.

The main strip had two grocery stores, two gas stations doubling as mechanic shops, a feed store, a
two-bay car wash, a post office, and a collection of
small shops: a thrift store, a boot-and-saddle repair,
and a general store selling ribbon, yoyos, school supplies, and a small selection of clothing when available.

Hotspur had a courthouse and city jail, one Police
Chief and a deputy sharing a single patrol car. The
water company office and a small farm and cattle
bureau office rounded out the town's administration.
Living in town meant being a mile or less from these
buildings. Houses sat on half-acre lots; some fenced,
some not. Older homes, two-story structures from
the late 1800s, still used their original barns and tool
sheds. Smaller, rundown homes also dotted the area.
Families with three or four children settled here, hoping for a wholesome, safe life.

Three churches served the community: Legacy Baptist, Covenant Church of Christ, and a small non-denominational, Fellowship Hall. A pavilion in the town square, funded by raffles, cake walks, school play tickets, and donations, hosted fairs and events. With growth, another pavilion might one day be needed.

The school building sat back on a hill outside town — a single, large structure housing kindergarten through seniors. Elementary grades outnumbered middle school, and middle outnumbered high school. One glance at the annual could show a ninth-grade class with twelve students, or a sophomore class with eight. Many of the teachers, superintendents, and pastors lived in town. Farming moms drove buses and worked in the cafeteria; a few teachers supplemented their income by driving a bus. Pastors also ran church buses, picking up congregants for Sunday services.

Hotspur sat on non-incorporated land, ninety minutes from either San Antonio or Austin depending on the back roads chosen. Developers hadn't reached this far yet, but growth in the bigger cities meant expansion was inevitable. People could only squeeze so many into one small town before it burst.

Texas. The second-largest state, a magnet for those from other places. Why not Alaska, with its wide-open spaces? Soon, the vast land around Hotspur would shrink under houses with zero lot lines, shoulder-to-shoulder neighbors, crowded roads, and drivers in a constant hurry. Technology would divide the world and engulf the town's simple way of life, threatening it with darkness never more to be.

But long before Hotspur's remarkable growth spurt, seeds of evil were already taking root.

6

"GREGG, HELP YOUR SISTER find her shoes, and Charlie, check the dogs' water bowls—make sure they're full," Lindy Koller hollered from the kitchen as she boxed up four bowls of homemade potato salad, two pans of Rice Krispies Treats, and a cooler of sweet tea.

She'd already loaded the hamburger meat, hot dogs with the buns, into the backseat of her 1979 GMC Suburban, known as 'Big Red,' the family ride. Big Red also hauled feed, seed, and kids; dogs to the vet, mom to town for groceries; and kids to see old Doc James.

Everything loaded up, kids in the back, Paul and Lindy in the front, and the family headed to the small downtown square of Hotspur, Texas, for the annual town summer fest.

––––––––––––

CHARCOAL AND GAS BARBECUES sat in rows on the sidewalks of the Pavilion. Lawn chairs and folding tables came out as women covered them with washable tablecloths and began putting out covered dishes—desserts, paper plates, cups, plastic cutlery, and napkins.

Kids ran to the playground where three swing sets, a merry-go-round, and a set of monkey bars sat, all donated by five of the more prominent families pooling their resources.

Behind the Pavilion, a wooden dance floor had been constructed for the event, and bales of hay provided the designated seating areas for attendees.

No band, but JJ of JJ's Dry Goods owned a nice stereo system and had it hooked up to speakers at the end. JJ's oldest son, a music freak, collected cassettes of every kind of music. One could expect bebop, jazz, rock-n-roll, or country tunes—not so much hip hop for this crowd.

The town gathered. Old friends saw old friends; kids who lived out of town met up with the town kids, many not seen in over a month—a lifetime to those in that age range.

A few older teens who owned horses gave other kids horseback rides. Some older boys, still without driver's licenses, had ridden in on small twin-cylinder Hondas or Suzukis. A few boys with real licenses rode larger bikes, taking pride without being ostentatious—they didn't pop wheelies or do donuts in the dirt.

Respectful, because parents were watching. Catch any of them out in a field without supervision, though, and they'd do scary things.

Doug Lewison braked to a stop, parking as close as possible to the Pavilion, as instructed by his bossy mother. She did not want to walk too far in this heat. "Texas heat—so different from California heat," she nagged. "The humidity in this state, heavens, and what it does to one's hair."

Her tinny voice grated on Doug, and he rolled his eyes. His father ignored her. Doug's after-statement

was always the same. "Then let's move back to California, not stay here in this hellhole."

That was when his father put in his two cents. "Now,
Douglas, we have more here than we did in California;
more to build on, too, and our dollar stretches far better. Ignore your mother's whining. She doesn't want to
move back." His father then gave her a nasty stare.

FIVE GIRLS SAT CHATTING, laughing, and discussing boys.
They saw Doug walking up with his older parents.
Kadie leaned toward her friends, her voice lowered.
"He is still so cute, even though he's sorta creepy."

"It's that California look—like a surfer boy. The
blonde hair and his light gray eyes, or is that light
blue?" Sheila asked the others.

"Iffin I ever get close enough to see what color they
are, I'll let you girls know," Holly Randolph said, her
hand in front of her mouth to hide her braces as she
snickered.

Audra Rafferty frowned, her head lowered, as she
cut her eyes over to Doug walking over to a table and
setting up a lawn chair for each parent, then returning
to the trunk.

"Gregg Koller hates the guy, hate-hates him. Says
he's a bully with a horrid mean streak; like a
hurt-you-and-not-care type of personality."

"Oh, you mean like he could hurt you, stuff you
in that trunk and toss you off a cliff?" Patty's eyes
widened in pretend fear, then she snorted a laugh.

"Well, you might be joking, Patty, but yeah, only
worse. Like he could do certain things to you."

Colleen's facial expression shifted to semi-fear. "I mean," she lowered her voice, eyes darting around, "like sexual stuff, and then get rid of you, and no one would find your body."

"Colleen Rayanne Dodge, have you been reading those scary nasty books again, I swear!" Kadie punched her in the arm.

"Well, it could happen. I heard this crap happens in smaller towns more than we hear about. Not just the big towns. Besides, big cities have more people—who'd know if anyone went missing? They've got so many people. Ain't like it'd be in Hotspur. One of us goes missing—everyone would know about it."

THE RESIDENTS OF HOTSPUR stuffed themselves with superb BBQ, corn on the cob, tater salad, baked beans, chips, cold green bean salad, and other dishes, including homemade cornbread. Adults relaxed under the cover of the Pavilion while kids scampered and played kick the can.

Some fifth- and sixth-graders set up a badminton net. Parents watched a white shuttlecock flying about, listening to the giggles.

"You think she's cute?" Berk Swanson nudged Gregg Koller, his eyes cutting over to Gloria Neeson.

"Sorta, I guess. She ain't my type, though."

A huff exited Berk's nose. "What, you mean you don't like the type that puts out, is that it, Koller?"

"Neeson puts out? Yeah, who do you know she's gone all the way with?"

"Kerry North."

"The guy from River Run? The superstar footballer?"

"Yep. He was at the stock show—him and I were girl watching—and he saw her with Holly and Audra. Says she was a nice piece of tail."

"God, Berk, and you believed him?"

This had the other two guys, Tye Slater and Preston Boedecker, in stitches.

Berk Swanson gave them all the eye and snarled. "Why's this so dang funny?"

"You honestly don't know, do you?" Gregg Koller asked.

"I guess not, so you wanna tell me?"

"Kerry North bats for the other side."

"What? He doesn't play baseball, he..." Only two seconds later, Berk's expression changed. "You mean he... uh... likes boys?"

"Yeah. I'm going out on a limb here and say he has never bedded Gloria Neeson. Now her brother, Jacob, might be a different story," said Gregg, brows wiggling.

"Jacob Neeson ever hears you say something like that, Gregg, and you better run—and never stop," Tye Slater interjected in a no-nonsense tone.

Sitting three tables away, heads bent together, Charlie, Bruce, Evan, and Neal were in deep discussion about the dance and who was off-limits to the others.

"Just because you said Lyssa Caldwell is pretty don't mean you got no claim on her, Geeze, Charlie."

"Look here, Bruce, I picked her before you did, so back off. If she doesn't like me, then you can ask her—but lemme try, okay?"

"Who will I ask then, creepy Nora?" A look of disgust landed on Bruce's chubby features.

"Hey, don't have to be a girl in our class, you jerk. Go a grade lower or higher. Seventh grade is short on girls, eighth grade short on boys, so it all works out, I think." Evan eyed the area, taking stock of the male/female ratio.

"Okay then, I pick Audra Rafferty."

Without a moment's thought, Evan Dyer flicked Neal Swanson's ear. "You already know I like her, so stop pissing me off."

Neal looked at the others and then cracked up. "I can't wait to see you and her slow dancing together, you being a foot shorter."

"Hey, I ain't stopped growing yet." Evan snuck a peek at Bruce's older sister. She was what made his heart sing.

—

FOUR BOYS, BEST OF friends through the thick of life. Sports, hunting, fishing, and girls—in that order at this age. The order of likes would change, and one day, girls would be at the top of the list; then again, as they aged, the order would adjust to fit their older selves.

—

THAT NIGHT, HE FELT the need to lash out, feeling unwelcome in this shitty, tiny town. In a few years, he figured he could just fly the coop—but not until his parents handed him over his trust fund. The idea of working a job did not appeal to the pampered, coddled only child.

His eyes scanned the area. The kids ran free; parents didn't pay attention. What sorts of terrible things happen in a small town?

None... they thought... in their town... Hotspur, Texas.

7

MR. AND MRS. LEWISON sat at the table alone until old lady Gilmore and old man Adair joined them, chatting them up. From the corner of his eye, Doug watched his arrogant parents. When he noticed his father laughing and a smile flit across his mother's face, it shocked the socks off him.

People in this cruddy town liked his parents. He'd already made his own bed with the kids his age; they no longer paid him any attention or gave him the time of day. They despised him, and he realized it was his own doing. A snort left his lips. If he wanted friends, he'd have to make friends with fourth graders, he thought to himself.

At the far back, four best friends sat on square hay bales, whispering and nudging each other, wondering who would ask a girl to dance first.

"Not a slow song," Charlie hissed. "Afraid my hands will get sweaty."

"Well, wipe 'em off on her shirt, she won't know," Bruce dared.

"Bruce, god, you ain't ever gonna get a girl, are you?"

A look of indignation crossed Bruce's face. "Not from here, they all know me. Maybe one day a girl from River Run will go out with me."

They all knew Bruce was right. He'd grossed out most of the Hotspur girls and had become the class clown. The thing was, Bruce was chubby, and the gals didn't think he was cute.

His extra layer of fat didn't bother the guys; it wasn't like any of them would kiss or hug him.

Charlie stood, squared his shoulders, and took a deep breath. "Okay, fellas, I'm going in."

Three sets of eyes followed Charlie Koller as he approached Lyssa Caldwell to ask for a dance.

Charlie's heart thudded, his breath caught in his throat, and a froggy, "Would you like to dance?" he croaked out.

A shy smile played on her lips. Her head ducked, she nodded and stood, and he took her hand, walking her to the dance floor.

His friends broke out with wide smiles, nodding and snickering.

Audra Rafferty sat alone, and Evan decided, why not? Better to give it a shot than do nothing. He stood.

"Hey, Dyer, where you off to?"

Evan turned with a heavy scowl. "To ask your sister to dance, you got a problem with that?"

Bruce feigned a hurt look. "Gosh, man, do what you gotta do. Hope it works out."

To the surprise of both Bruce and Neal, Audra Rafferty accepted the offer to dance with Evan. When Audra wasn't looking, Evan stuck his tongue out at his friends.

All this newfound bravery had Neal up on his feet. He asked Holly to dance, and once the small makeshift dance floor was full, kids of all ages with flailing arms and feet, Bruce Rafferty got up and danced too.

Parents sat in groups of men and women. Women discussed gardens, canning, cooking, and raising chickens, while men discussed livestock and planting. Water drainage issues had caused some concerns in certain low-lying areas with the last heavy rain, and there was the possibility of no rain for months.

"I gotta drain a tank, got algae growing, it's going to be a mess," Len Dyer spat out a stream of tobacco juice.

Paul Koller asked, "Can't you pull the plug?"

"So, Len," Oren Rafferty added, "why will it be a mess?"

"Because it's a natural tank, the one closest to Bea's chicken coop, and god, have I heard about not making her hen house a wet mess."

The other men nodded, silent condolences for his unhappy wife.

"How about digging a ditch, then damming it up to move the water flow away from the coops?"

Doug listened in, leaning against the posts supporting the pavilion. Snoozefest. Hotspur must be the most boring place ever.

His gaze traveled back to his parents, sitting relaxed and conversing with folks closer to their age.

Escape. He needed to get away and think. First, he stopped at the car and fished the flashlight out of the glove box, shoving it in his back pocket. If he were walking at night, he would need it.

He strolled past the two-bay car wash, Post Office, and a blinking yellow light, then vanished into the darkness.

He felt ready to start his hunt. He'd spent part of the fall on horseback familiarizing himself with the state roads and the numbers. At first, it had been confusing and seemed complex; then he figured if these hay-seed farmers could get around, then he could, too.

A few times he'd taken his father's truck for a spin, driving up and down various roads, recording the locations of side roads that led to nowhere, dead ends that marked the absolute end of any discernible path. These were roads less traveled, and thus, ideas formed. Step one: find a place. Check. Step two: get a victim. Harder to do than he'd figured. Okay, if he could find a victim, he would plan steps three and four... maybe even step five, just for fun.

"THANK YOU FOR DANCING with me, Lyssa," said Charlie.

"Uh, sure, and uh, thanks for asking me," she said, her voice tiny.

The music slowed, and Charlie confidently put his arm around her waist and pulled her a little closer. Lyssa draped an arm over his shoulder and around his neck, and he felt her body relax.

"You missed where you used to live?"

"Shreveport? No, not really."

"Mrs. Sutton said your family is military."

"Uh, yeah, my dad was in the army."

"He ain't no more?"

Lyssa Caldwell's eyes teared up and she swayed her head. Charlie felt like a fool. He'd made her cry, and this was uncharted territory for a 12-year-old farm boy.

"Oh, God, I... I'm sorry, Lyssa, I... oh shoot!" He took her hand and led her over to an empty stack of hay, sitting her down. She covered her face and cried, and he sat beside her, putting an arm over her shoulder, trying to comfort her.

"I'm, oh, I'm so sorry, I didn't mean to cry like a titty-baby, Charlie."

"Uh, it's okay, I understand."

She smiled a watery smile. "No, no you don't. You must think my dad is dead, is that it?"

"Ain't he?"

Again, Lyssa shook her head. "He and my mom are divorcing. He stayed in Shreveport, he's still active in the army. My mom has a sister who lives in River Run and, well, she offered to help us out, but mom wanted to do this on her own. She picked Hotspur because she lived here a long time ago. She says she has fun memories of this place. My grandpa—my mom's dad—used to own a huge cattle ranch out here. Uh, have you ever heard of the Red Oak Ranch?"

Charlie's eyes widened. "Uh-huh, sure have. My dad told me twenty or thirty years ago it was the biggest horse and cattle ranch in these parts; but the farmhouse, barn, and everything burned to the ground."

Lyssa let out a sigh. "I've heard the story a lot," she chuckled. "Lightning hit the barn and took it all. Way before I was born. My grandma died in the fire, guess that had to be the worst of it all. Anyway, after that, grandpa gave up, sold off the cattle and all the livestock, then parceled out the land and sold it all."

She eyed Charlie, who ducked his head.

"It's okay, Charlie, I know your granddad bought some of my grandpa's old ranch land and your dad owns it now."

"Gosh, I'm sorry, Lyssa, what awful luck. Only I am happy your mom came back to Hotspur."

He took her hand in a brave move and laced his fingers with hers.

Evan sat with Audra Rafferty, laughing at the things she told him about Bruce. He'd be ready with comebacks for when Bruce started teasing him. His heart still pounded watching Audra's pretty face, hoping she might like him, just a little.

Neal and Holly shared a Coke and some cookies and talked about her pregnant horse who was about to foal. She invited Neal to come over when Matilda was ready to give birth, if he wanted to.

Bruce sat with three of the boys he knew from seventh grade who rode the bus with them. It didn't matter who was who, or who was older or younger; this was a community hinged on friendships.

8

Doug whipped out the flashlight as the town's lights faded behind him. He was a considerable distance from home, yet it didn't bother him. If he stayed on the main road, his parents would drive past on their way home.

Darkness. Crud, it was dark, and he hoped his prehistoric father didn't run him down.

A coyote howled.

Okay, yep, he should have thought this through. He hadn't thought about needing a weapon, like a shotgun, to protect himself from the wilds.

This made him snicker. Who would protect his victims from him?

There was no way he'd go back to killing animals. That ship had sailed.

His first victim sailing away made him laugh. She'd sailed away, hooked to metal on a tanker.

Doug's laughter died as he focused on the question of who he'd take. It could be no one from Hotspur. Not yet, anyway. He'd have to locate a person from another town, or a vagrant, or a runaway.

Crap. It wasn't like they were out here in droves, like they were in San Francisco. Patience. He would need to scope it out more, get the right victim.

He wanted a girl. But if it had to be a guy, then, well, it would have to be.

His feet were hurting, so he waved his light around to find a place to rest. He watched the road, watching for his parents' Lincoln.

Doug sat, his back against the post of a fence. He propped up the flashlight, aiming at the street, so that anyone driving by would see the stream of light and investigate. Or he hoped they did.

His eyes closed, and his thoughts fell back three years, to the day he turned thirteen.

———

"MAN, DOUG, YOU GOT pretty neat parents."

A dark look crossed the birthday boy's face. "No, I don't, Ryan. I got old geezer parents, and it's a drag."

"Look at the stuff they buy you. Don't that count for nothing?"

"Oh sure. Terrific to have stuff, I guess," Doug's reply sounded morose.

He envied Ryan, who had a dad who played basketball, football, and coached his baseball team. His dad, an old man, no longer ran or played childish games.

Vacations were never at the beach. They were at five-star hotels, art galleries, or museums. Every boy needed refinement and to learn to be proper.

"Douglas," his mother called out, "time to cut the cake and serve."

"Come on, let's go get cake and ice cream, Dougie. Then ask your dad if you can come to our house. I got two new video games for my Atari: Missile Command and Major League Baseball."

"Yeah, but I gotta wait for everyone else to leave first. My mother will have a hissy fit if I leave and other kids are still here."

Other kids. They weren't his real friends. Just classmates his mother invited to his birthday party to make a show of it. Balloons, a clown, bags of goodies for each kid.

His mother even planned a stupid contest with the prize of four movie theater tickets, including popcorn and sodas.

William Thatcher won the tickets, which pleased his parents. The contest was about who could name the most state capitals in two minutes.

Doug didn't like William, Les, Craig, Erin, Rhonda, Corey, or any of the kids his mother invited. They were all from well-off families, just as haughty as she was.

His dad, well, Pop liked to brag, and so did the other fathers. A bunch of old windbags.

"Douglas, I think Les wanted you to come over to his house. His mother invited you."

Mrs. Lewison sounded disappointed that her son would rather spend time with Ryan Chapin.

The Chapins were poor, and Arthur and Camille Lewison couldn't understand why Douglas was so drawn to this boy. But Ryan was the child Doug preferred to spend time with, so they allowed the friendship to blossom, despite their trepidations.

———

"THESE ARE PRETTY COOL games, ain't they?" Ryan beamed.

"I wish my parents would let me get video games."

Ryan looked at his best friend, eyes wide. "Gosh, Doug, they get you anything you want, so why not get them for you?"

"Because my dad says it is a pure waste of time and I should be concentrating on what my future is. And it ain't playing games."

"Well," Ryan said, popping in another game called Asteroids, and handing Doug a joystick, "my dad says this sorta technology is our future and I should learn all about it."

Doug wished Ryan was his brother, and they had the same dad.

It had been devastating news two years later. Ryan and his family were moving away. Out of Doug's life.

Santa Cruz County and San Joaquin County were 107 miles apart. Mr. and Mrs. Lewison couldn't have been happier that the Chapin boy was out of their son's life.

Doug Lewison sunk into a dark depression. Ryan was that one friend who never asked questions, never judged him, and just because he came from a wealthy family, never used him to get things.

Ryan was a genuine friend. One who laughed, kidded, and shared secrets and dreams.

Some boys didn't like Ryan because he was poor. The rest didn't like Doug because he was rich. For these two boys, there had been no happiness in between.

———————

AT AGE THIRTEEN, DOUG had already killed.

It was a satisfying feeling, watching the life drain from a being.

His first time was a stray dog. An animal no one would miss.

The next one was a feral cat. That had been tough. The feline acted wild, and he'd gotten scratched.

Killing that nasty varmint was more than satisfying. Revenge for him that day felt sweet. He duct-taped the creature's mouth, tortured the squalling animal, inflicting pain for his satisfying payback.

After dumping the dead carcass down the street sewage drain, he went home and doctored his wounds, hoping like heck he didn't get rabies or an infection.

Once it healed, there had been a faint scar left. His first trophy.

Over the summer, he nabbed neighbors' various pets: cats, dogs, ferrets, and a few rabbits. Doug never got caught.

He found the lost pet posters hilarious. 'Have you seen Spike, or Fluffy? If you do, please call—reward!'

Not once in his years had he ever asked his parents for a puppy or a kitten. Thank goodness he hadn't.

***

The girl, though. She was upping his game.

He was fourteen, only there was maturity to Doug's facial features, hinting at an age exceeding his true years.

It was the summer of his eighth-grade year.

That night, he'd found her and flashed a little money. Easy enough to get her attention.

She slinked up to him, crooning the things she could do to him.

Still being a virgin, no way he would do the deed for the first time with a streetwalking drug addict.

The other issue was the scare of HIV and AIDS. Nope. Better safe and live another day.

Anyway, the killing was a sexual satisfaction he'd never experienced until that night. Now he had something to look forward to—or so he thought—until the day his parents packed up their lives and moved out here to BFE.

Doug took the flashlight and shined the light on his left forearm. The white skinny scar from where the cat scratched him was still visible. He smiled at the memory.

Gravel crunched under tires, and he stood, stepping to the rim of the road. He waved the light, hoping to stop the driver.

The car came to a stop. He saw it was his parents' vehicle.

His father rolled the window down. His mother leaned into the driver's area. Her expression twisted.

"Douglas! You have had us worried to death. Get in the car."

His father repeated her words. "Get in the car."

The rest of the drive home was him getting bawled out. He apologized for scaring years off their lives.

Man, the thought of shaving years off their lives, if only it were possible, brought a sinister smile to his face.

9

IT WAS 1983.

The move.

Culture shock.

From a large modern city to a rural piece of dirt and no life.

"Why are we moving?"

Camille Lewison looked up at her son, an incredulous look crossing her face.

"Like you don't know, Douglas."

"I only have three more years of high school, and I do not want to move."

Doug crossed his arms over his chest; his feet planted in a wide stance. He didn't care about leaving friends. All he cared about was having to leave his hunting grounds and his hidden darkness.

"Your father thinks it's best to move us out of the state. Well, so do I."

"All because of one stupid lie? Are you ever going to believe me?" His voice carried through the expansive house.

"Douglas Gordon Lewison, do not raise your voice to me." Her tone was that of an army drill sergeant, and her eyes darkened.

Arthur Lewison stormed into the room. "What are you two yelling about?"

"Well, dear, I will give you two guesses. Douglas wants to stay. And I said no."

"Douglas, wait for me in the den."

The boy stood steadfast, his feet unmoving, his expression full of hatred.

"I ... said ... go ..." his father's words measured, and Doug popped out with, "Yeah, I heard you. I'm going."

His stride yielded purpose as he yanked the doorknob and slammed it shut behind him. The bang rattled the door frame, jarring his mother's already stretched nerves.

Arthur sat beside his wife, whose eyes welled with tears, and covered her small, wrinkled hand with his own age-spotted one.

"Art, we can't lose our son. I never thought we'd have him, so I won't lose him."

"Cammie," he called her his pet-name, "a fresh start for him. For us, it's the best I can do. This evil side of our boy, I just don't understand it."

"It's our fault, Art. We indulged him too much."

"Camille Drake Lewison, it is not our fault, but if something else happens, and we don't get him out of California, then yes, it will be our fault."

———

DOUG HEARD THEM THROUGH the vents—his favorite way to listen to his parents' private conversations.

How much did they know, and who the heck had seen him or knew what he'd done?

He suspected it was his art teacher because of the drawings, or maybe his English teacher because of the poems and short stories. It was all in his imagination; none of it was real, he'd explained.

A creative, mysterious psyche, his dark side; like Edgar Allan Poe, or Mary Shelley, shoot, even Bram Stoker. Souls with malevolent stories stirring inside their minds, just like him.

Doug continued to listen.

"His attitude about it all—it bothers me, and I'm a little afraid of him."

Doug smiled—good, he thought.

"Art, you don't mean that."

Mom, ever the hopeful one—Doug smirked at her tone.

"Honey, did you watch him at the Van de Bern's daughter's funeral?" Art sounded like he was complaining.

His face grew dark as he continued to listen.

"No, I, well, I couldn't. That poor girl's mother, I just ..." Camille held her hands up in defeat.

"The police said there's no proof Doug was there, but in my heart, Cammie, I feel, well, I don't know what I feel."

She wiped her eyes and stood, straightening her dress, and she patted her hair. "A fresh start, Art. Small town life. Texas might be what our son needs."

Doug moved away from the vent—hating them even more.

———

THREE DAYS AFTER THE summer festival.

"Mom, who is that kid out by the barn?" Doug moved the curtains, enough to see but not enough to be seen.

"I think he's a runaway. Mr. Grist says he picked him up hitchhiking on his way back from the feed store."

"What's Mr. Grist's plan on doing with him?"

In his late thirties, maybe forty, hard to say, Harry Grist was the handyman, yardman, all-around gofer for the Lewisons, and a bit of a dunce, as Arthur said.

"Don't know. Listen, Doug, we need to discuss college; it's only a few years away, you know."

"Got no plans to go to any college."

"Doug, your father and I feel like the University of Texas in Austin is the perfect choice. It's only ninety miles from Hotspur, so it'll be easy for you to come home for a visit. Of course, you'll want to live on campus, or we can find you student housing. Dad and I aren't getting any younger, and, well, it'd be nice to have you close."

She never listened—neither of them did.

He had no desire to go to college, none. Why did he need schooling?

He was their only heir—he'd get the dough once they kicked the bucket, which for him would not be soon enough.

"...It's been nice and calm here, and we have grown attached to this place, and, well, have you decided on who you're taking?" His mother rambled on.

Her son wasn't paying attention to her. His eyes were on the scrawny young boy out by the toolshed with Mr. Grist and his dad.

"Doug, did you hear me?"

He let out a silent huff of anger. "No, Mom, what did you say?"

"I wanted to know if you have a girl in mind for the school dance?"

Her son's face wrinkled in disgust, question, and amusement.

"Prom? No. And if I go, who would go with me? I'm not a dancer, and it doesn't matter because none of the girls are interested in me."

"How about we throw a party, invite your class, a few of the younger kids too, and we ..."

Doug cut her off with an abrupt slice of his hand.

"No. No party." With that, he walked to the front door, slamming it shut behind him.

Camille Lewison's lips quivered; her son's anger festered; she saw it in his face, body language, and attitude.

He hated his life; he hated them; and he hated Texas; but he could never return to California.

Another fresh start for her son would be college life—meeting more people; maybe meeting a new best friend. He hadn't had one since Ryan Chapin.

Her son never had a steady girlfriend, or many friends, for that matter. He wasn't ugly, but his personality made him unattractive to everyone.

GORDON DRAKE AND HIS wife, Lucinda Harris Drake, both dead.

Lucinda went stark raving mad when Doug was eleven months old. She murdered Gordon in his sleep, then hung herself.

A week after their funerals, it was then that Arthur and Camille took their nephew Douglas, completed all the adoption paperwork, and moved from Boston to California ... for ... a fresh start.

10

"WOW, I CAN'T BELIEVE we did it."

Charlie stood back, his eyes shining with pride.

The treehouse was complete.

With the help of his dad, they'd constructed a grand fort.

There was railing around the sides. They'd put up a secondary ladder so they could enter the structure from either side of the tree, and built a sentry's post up just a few feet higher.

Although not enclosed all the way around, they had fabricated a roof using old shingles Paul had left over after repairing the farmhouse's roof last spring. Paul and Lindy Koller enjoyed finding new uses for old things; this included old asphalt shingles.

"You think we can build a table and connect it here?" Charlie pointed to the side rail.

"Charlie Boy, I don't see why not, and it looks like there's enough lumber left. You can use half pieces of plywood for the top. Okay, fellas, I gotta head back—got some calves to vaccinate, yet."

"Dad." Charlie landed a hand on his father's arm.

"Yeah, son?"

"Thank you for this. We love it, don't we, fellas?"

Bruce, Neal, and Evan grinned, their smiles wide and boyish. "Yes, Mr. Koller, we love it, and thanks."

Paul ruffled his son's sandy-brown head and winked. "I expect an invitation to your first camp out."

Excitement shone in Charlie's eyes, his face aglow. "Oh man, that'd be awesome, Dad."

*

They spent summer days doing chores, playing at their new fort, and swimming in the tank.

Weekends were chaotic, with the boys sleeping over at each other's houses, driving their older siblings crazy, and chasing away the younger ones.

Homemade pizzas or burgers on the grill.

The Swansons had a VHS player, and the boys saved their chore money to rent movies for the summer.

Three times during the summer, Meg Rafferty, Lindy Koller, Bea Dyer, and Claudia Swanson took three car-loads of kids to Marble Falls to the public swimming pool.

A wild hour-and-a-half car ride, with kids all talking and laughing; boys squaring off on which girl was theirs before the adventure.

They swam, woofed down hot dogs cooked on the park grills, ate chips, cookies, and other various picnic foods, and drank sodas.

After the summer fest in town, Charlie claimed Lyssa as his girlfriend, and she had no objections.

Neal and Holly became an item; and much to Evan's heartbreak, a tenth grader named Tye Slater claimed Audra Rafferty as his girl.

Bruce, still clumsy with the fairer sex, continued to be the class clown year-round ... for now.

The ride back was much quieter.

Tired, sun-drenched, and waterlogged, kids sat—some nodding off, others chatting more sedately—and boys held their girls' hands, content in their newfound puppy love.

"What a fun day. I'm so happy you invited me, Charlie," Lyssa glowed, her nose pink from too much sun.

"Me too. I mean, I had a fantastic time today, too. I hope you get to go again." Charlie gave her hand a gentle squeeze.

"Oh? When will you go again?"

"One more time this year, and the last time we get to stay and go to the six o'clock movie. It'll be right before school starts. You think your mom will say yes?" Charlie sent up a silent prayer.

"I think she will, but I might have to bring my little brother next time."

"What's his name again?"

"Danny, and he's eight and a pill." She huffed.

"Well, my little sister Libby," his head gestured to the little girl asleep on his mom's shoulder in the second-row seating of the SUV, "she's almost nine. She and Danny might have fun together."

"Maybe. Danny's a little weird. He's not much of an outdoorsy kid."

This had Charlie laughing. "Well, let him hang out with Libby, and he'll be mud wrestling and chasing chickens in no time."

For the rest of the ride, they talked about the new school year and engaged in animated conversations with Neal, Holly, and Evan, snickering at Bruce's antics.

Summer flew, and the new school year was about to begin.

11

In that same summer, on the Lewison's fancy spread.

The new kid, Doug, the unease he felt, drove him into a dark place. All he dreamed of was being back in the Bay Area—sand, surf, and everything he knew his entire life. He hated Texas, his parents, and his life.

No friends. He was alone.

Doug puttered around with his horse, riding, and scheming. He needed to find something that made him feel good. His parents only pushed him, suggesting he should entertain friends here on their fancy homestead.

He balked at the idea, diving deeper into his solitude, retreating as far from them as he could emotionally.

Mr. Grist had taken the runaway under his wing and was caring for him. Feeding him and letting him be his shadow at the Lewison's. He'd learned the kid's name and where he was from. Marlin Hudson. He'd run away from his home in Monahans, Texas, headed to San Antonio.

Doug checked the map. From Monahans to Hotspur was about 230 miles, and then over another hundred to San Antonio. After cornering Mr. Grist while the youth was off doing a chore, Doug learned that Marlin had taken a Greyhound bus partway and had hitch-hiked the rest of the time.

"He's trying to find his old man," Grist said, "says his mom's a junkie and won't notice he's left. Got a brother and sister, one younger and one older; they stayed with the mom."

"How old is he?" Doug asked, trying to sound less interested than he was.

"Thirteen," Grist replied. "I reckon to pay him some wages for doing work around here, then drive him down to Junction, let him get a bus to San Antonio so he can find his old man."

"Huh, mighty nice of you, isn't it, Mr. Grist?"

The man scowled. "Well, I guess I could ask your rich daddy to fork over some cash to help the kid, but I believe a boy needs to learn responsibility for his actions." His eyebrows arched at Doug.

"And what's that supposed to mean, you trying to tell me something?"

"Nope, just saying, that's all." Grist chawed his tobacco and spit out a wad of brown juice at Doug's feet, avoiding the tips of his boots by mere millimeters. "Now, I gotta get back to earning my pay."

Harry Grist turned and walked to the barn, leaving Doug scowling at his backside.

Late that afternoon, upstairs in his room, Doug used his field glasses to watch Grist and Marlin finish chores. They clowned around, laughing. Mr. Grist squirted him with the hose he used to clean out the horse trough.

The lad got him back, flicking off Harry's hat and running off with it. All in fun.

It was when the old guy draped an arm over the gangly teenager's shoulder that stirred an emotion in the other boy.

In a short two weeks, the ragged runaway teen and their handyman bonded.

It ticked Doug off. Harry Grist never gave him the time of day, and this galled Doug to no end.

Plenty of times he'd been outside while Mr. Grist worked and did chores. Not once had the man tried to befriend him or act friendly. No horsing around or joking. Just warnings to stay out of the way and not get hurt.

Grist treated him with kid-gloves, like a porcelain doll or an ugly, unlovable old mutt.

This caused a hatred which stirred deep within Doug. Could be because not once in his life had he bonded with anyone ... except Ryan Chapin.

He wished once again that Ryan had been his brother, and he was still in California, even if it wasn't near the water. That was where his heart belonged.

Doug detested other people having happiness when he was here with zero joy in his life. He needed that joy. He knew where his enjoyment was.

He moved the drapes over, then placed the binoculars back in the leather case, snapping it shut.

He lay on his bed, his arms under his head, and closed his eyes.

That county road, five miles out, the one that flooded every time it rained hard.

The road led to the rear of old man Adair's back fifteen acres and a barbed wire fence. Doug was certain Adair owned the property. However, that area was always undisturbed. He'd been watching for months.

After a small patch of land got cleared, Adair moved all the limbs and dead brush into a heap and stopped whatever project he'd been planning.

Marlin had shown an interest in horses. Maybe it was time for a riding lesson. Get him and the old man all comfy with the idea.

In a few weeks, maybe Marlin would just take his measly earnings and run off again.

The riding lessons went well. Grist's worries about Doug and his ulterior motives waned.

In less than four weeks, school would be starting. Grist wanted Marlin to enroll so he wouldn't be passing up on an education.

Doug knew Grist had a soft spot for the runaway. He'd said Marlin reminded him of himself at that age.

Grist's childhood was similar. A mom who drank herself into oblivion, and his father had run off. He had run away when he was ten but never found his father.

What Harry Grist hoped was that Marlin would stay put and live in Hotspur, having a chance at a regular life.

Huh—not if Doug had his way. Ripping the life from the boy and the happiness out from under Harry Grist—that was his plan.

Doug was brushing down his gelding. Marlin excitedly recounted their recent lesson and how Doug let him run his pony at a gallop.

"You know, Mr. Harry," the lad called him by his first name, but with respect, adding in the "Mister," "I sure will miss this place and the animals, 'specially the pony I been a riding. But I need to find my dad."

"You know, boy, if your pop says you gotta go back to Monahans to live with your mom, then you got money to either get back, or if you want, you can come back here and stay a spell."

A sneer covered Doug's face. Grist's newfound affection and fatherly attitude toward the skinny teenage runaway infuriated him. He felt a twinge of jealousy.

The fact was, Harry Grist never gave him that type of attention ... and he wondered why not.

He received the same cool, distant affection from his parents and their aging California acquaintances.

Some days, the repulsion he felt for himself was a physical force, pushing him down, making him want to disappear.

When days like this hovered over him, a dark cloud drove that inner demon to wake and demand a release.

He hadn't wished to become a monster. However, it felt like something had thrust this innate action upon him against his will. How and by whom, he did not understand.

But he did not want it controlled, nor caged. This was what freed his happiness.

Marlin whined about being enrolled in school. If he was at school, he wasn't earning money by doing chores. Since Mr. Grist paid him per chore completed, this was another strange thing to Doug.

"Mr. Harry, I'll have enough money if I keep working, so I don't wanna go to school here. I'll go when I get to San Antonio, I promise."

Harry Grist would not argue with the young man. He could do chores in the morning before school, come home to do homework, then finish his chores before dinner. He'd earn a little less, but he'd still be earning and saving.

If he made decent grades, he'd get compensated for that, too.

This argument went on for three days. An unhappy Marlin stomped around the barn and tack house, doing his chores, but with anger.

"One semester, you finish that, and I'll give you your cash, and you can take off for San Antonio after that, any time you want," Harry informed the teenager in a no-nonsense tone.

If Marlin wanted his wages, he'd have to go along with Harry's deal.

This was when Doug formed his nefarious plot.

12

HE BAITED THE YOUNGSTER. "School starts in six days, you ready?"

"No, I sure ain't. I ain't even got new duds to wear, and don't care about going. Just want to get to San Antonio, then see what my pop has going on."

"Take the money you have and leave then." Doug's words were nonchalant.

"Can't."

"Why not?"

"Mr. Harry has my money hidden from me."

"What if I knew where it was, would that help you?" Doug again acted like the boy's friend.

"You do? Where?"

"How will you get to the bus stop if you get the cash?"

Marlin squinted, thinking. "Can you drive me?"

Doug shook his head. "Grist will get mad at me. I can't do it. But, hey, why don't you saddle the pony and go for a ride?"

"Are you crazy? I can't ride that pony to San Antonio—they'll arrest me for stealing a horse. Uh-uh, no way, man."

"No, listen. Mr. Grist will ask me to go looking for you when you don't come back. You wait for me, and I'll find the pony. See, and tell the old guy you must'a have thumbed a ride since I couldn't find you anywhere."

Marlin's brows dipped. "I don't know, Doug."

"Fine by me. I don't care one way or the other," his words drifting away like smoke. "But Mr. Harry's will make you go to school if you stay, ain't no way around that."

He thought for a minute. If he had the cash, then it'd work out. He'd saved enough for a bus ticket and then some. If his dad didn't want him, then maybe Mr. Harry would let him come back.

"Okay, I'll do it."

Doug smiled, his brows arched up. His heart raced, his insides tingled. He laid out the plan. He instructed Marlin to meet him on the old road that flooded out, the one that ended at the barbed wire fence line at Glen Adair's property.

"I'll get the money he has stashed," Doug lied. "Tonight, after your chores, an hour before sundown, saddle up Milly. Tell Harry you need to think about this school stuff, and riding is relaxing. He'll understand you gotta have some time to make a choice. When you don't come back, he'll ask me to find you. You sure you can do this?"

The youngster nodded. He stared at his feet. "I don't got no other choices since he won't give me the cash I've already earned unless I go to stupid school."

"Good. It's a plan. See you later. You'd better get to your chores until then."

Doug watched a sullen Marlin Hudson walk back toward the barn to find Harry Grist.

How easy it was to set his victim up—and how much happiness he'd soon release for himself.

———

"Was getting worried you weren't coming with my greenbacks. Thought you were going to leave me here with my thumb up my butt like an idiot," Marlin tried, sounding tough, but there was a quaver in his voice, not missed by Doug.

"Yeah, had to wait until the old guy wasn't looking to get your cash." Again, Doug was less than honest.

Marlin stood and patted the soft muzzle of the pony. "I'll miss this here filly, and this place. But, well, maybe one day I'll come back, bring my dad so he can tell Mr. Harry thanks for helping me out."

Doug tied his horse to the barbed wire fence next to where the boy had the pony tied.

"Hey, uh, Doug, uh, aren't you taking me to the main road, then come back and get the pony, telling everyone I hightailed it?"

He pursed his lips in a sorta frown. "I was, but changed my mind. I got a better idea."

With a thoughtful expression, Marlin folded his twig-like arms and said, "You do? Okay, I'm listening."

"First, let me get you your wages. I mean, you worked hard for the money."

"Yeah, be needing it for a bus ticket, thanks, Doug."

"Oh, no need to thank me," Doug said, sticking a hand inside the worn-out leather pannier. His back to the youth, he tugged out a roll of duct tape and stuck it under his shirt, shoving it beneath the waistband of his jeans.

Next, he pulled out a zippered money bag. Then he turned and walked the few feet to face Marlin.

"Here you are, Marlin, your ticket home."

Marlin held the bag, unzipping it. He saw loose bills, and a smile flitted across his face. "Oh, my, this is ... Wait, what the, Doug! No."

Doug smacked the boy with the side of his hard leather riding crop, sending him sprawling sideways—and then pounced.

It was too easy. The gangly teen was bony, with no muscle power. Marlin stood about five foot seven, stick thin at about 120 pounds. Doug stood six feet, weighing right at 170. He crushed the boy.

The duct tape peeled off, making a hissing sound of zzz-zwwaack, as he ripped a piece off the roll.

Marlin's eyes were full of fear. Doug's body weight pinned him down. With a sudden jerk, he hoisted the boy's thin arms above his head, secured his wrists with tape, then planted a foot on Marlin's torso, his heavier weight keeping him down.

The unzipped bag of cash had fallen to the ground, and a few bills floated out. With his foot, Doug nudged the bag over, not caring about that.

At his feet lay his prize—a human so scared he struggled to breathe.

"Stop whimpering and take breaths through your nose, you fool."

He yanked the boy up, eyeing him from his head to his dirty tennis shoes.

"Not my first pick, but hey, beggars cannot be choosy, can they?"

Marlin's knees quaked, and when Doug looked down, the boy peed his pants.

"Gross, kid. But it'll dry out."

Doug dragged Marlin to a larger tree and had him sit with his back against the trunk. He taped his ankles together with duct tape. "Don't run off. I'll be back in a jiff," Doug added with a tiny laugh at his own joke.

Out of the pannier, he pulled a thin chain and a padlock. At the end, he looped it into the barbed wire fence, then looped the other end to a shackle. He snapped it on Marlin's wrist, padlocking the ends as tightly as he could.

"No one comes out here, but I gotta keep your mouth taped shut. Can't have you yelling for help, now, can I? After I let Harry know you up and run away again, he might come looking for you—but he'd never come out here since he thinks you're off to find your daddy in San Antonio. When I get back tonight, you and I will have a bit of fun. And Marlin, well, I just can't wait."

Doug's smile was cruel, and the tiny laugh sent chills up Marlin's spine.

Then the older boy was on his horse, leading a riderless pony to Lewison's big fancy house.

Trapped. No way to scream. No way to run.

The boy was a nobody, a runaway—and it seemed no one was looking for him. Marlin had made the horrific decision that led him to a path of unimaginable horror. He should have never left Monahans, Texas.

13

HARRY GRIST RUBBED HIS neck. "He just left the pony and took off? With no money?"

He walked over to his hiding place and pulled out the canvas bag he'd shoved into an old toolbox under the top tray. "It's gone. How'd that kid know I hid it here?"

Harry Grist lifted his hat, then lowered it in a nervous, worried gesture. "Can't believe he'd just up and leave like that, don't understand it."

Doug said, shrugging, "Guess you making him go to school gave him his reasons to run off."

"I'm driving up to the main road, try to find the stupid kid afore he gets himself killed by someone running his skinny hind end over. You come with me; help me look while I drive." If something happened to that boy, Harry would never forgive himself.

"Oh, uh, sure, let me get a flashlight, it'll be too dark to see soon."

The feigned concern in Doug's eyes and the gentle touch on the old man's arm was enough to throw him off his trail.

Mr. Grist cranked the old truck to life and looked at Doug. "Where did you say you found the pony?"

Doug misled the old guy, leading him toward the Koller ranch, six miles south of where he left Marlin, trapped and frightened.

———

"THIS IS WHERE YOU found Milly?" Mr. Grist stopped the truck but didn't kill the engine.

Doug pointed. "Yeah, Marlin tied her up in the bramble. Guess he was trying to hide her. Never figured he'd let her get hurt. What if she'd broken free and got hit by a car or truck in the dark?"

Harry Grist turned his head, his lips set in a scowl. "She would have found her way home. It's the kid I'm worried about, not that pony."

"Yeah, sure, sorry. Look, from here about a mile up is a main crossroad, betcha he hitched a ride."

The sound of wheels crunching gravel and dust rolling up as Paul Koller's truck approached. He slowed to a stop and rolled down the window.

"Truck problems?"

The man stepped over and stuck his hand out. "No, it's running fine. Harry Grist, we've met a few times before, years back. I work for the Lewison's now."

Sticking his truck in park then engaging the emergency brake, Paul stepped out, grabbing Grist's outstretched hand. "Nice to see you again. Can I help with anything?"

Paul Koller pursed his lips.

"Yeah, on your drive in did you see a kid, about five foot six, skinny, wearing faded jeans and a red T-shirt? He'd a been walking that direction towards the main blacktop."

"No, we didn't. That's my son Charlie." Koller's eyes went to the truck where Charlie sat in the passenger's seat. "We drove in from River Run to pick up some feed. You want us to help look for him?"

"Two more sets of eyes be mighty helpful." Grist nodded, his face etched in worry.

Paul Koller hollered to his son. "Charlie, check the glove box. Do we got a flashlight in there, the batteries still good?"

Charlie popped open the glove compartment and withdrew a heavy-duty flashlight, switched it on, and shined the beam out the window. "Yep, batteries are working fine."

He got out and stood by his dad.

"Tell you what, Harry, me and my boy will drive back and take the left junction road, go down about five miles; and turn back and scope out the corn field, he might 'a stayed off the road in the dark."

Harry Grist's head bobbed. "Yep, and me and Doug will go the opposite direction, and work our way toward town. He can't have gotten too far on foot."

Doug said, "We're sunk if the brat, er, uh, kid hitch-hiked, he'll be long gone by now."

"We didn't pass any vehicles on our way in, did we dad?" Charlie looked up expectantly at his father.

"No, and unless the youngster crossed a field to get to the main road, we should've seen him. About how long you say he's been gone?"

Grist thought for a minute, then said, "I reckon about two and a half hours, that what you think Doug?"

"Maybe longer. He took the pony about two hours ago and might be closer to three."

"Let's get started. How about we meet you back here, okay, Mr. Koller?"

"Paul, call me Paul, and sure, we'll meet you back here."

NO SIGN OF THE boy. Neither of the two-man search parties had seen hide nor hair of a thin 14-year-old boy wearing a faded red t-shirt and jeans. At this time of the evening, they had passed zero cars; no one was out and about on these desolate country roads; they were all home. With the day's work done, the country folk attended their evening chores, enjoying a hearty dinner before settling down to snuggle in for the night.

Harry fretted, and wanted to tan that boy's rear-end, but if he couldn't find him, then what was the old guy to do?

"Thanks for helping us, Paul. Very nice of y'all to take the time." Grist looked at Charlie. "You what, thirteen?"

"No, sir, not for another month."

"Marlin, the kid that ran off, he's fourteen. I sure hope he finds his way to his Pa in San Antonio. Boy's need their dad, and that boy, well, I just hope he's safe. If he got a ride, pretty sure it was nice folks that carried him to the Greyhound station. Thanks again." The man shook hands with Paul and said, "Come on Doug."

Paul and Charlie got into the truck and seat belted in.

"Man, dad, it'd be sorta scary out here at night, you know, plenty of hungry coyotes, and what if he steps on a rattler?" Charlie shuddered.

"Well, Charlie Boy, if that kid hitched from Monahans to here, seems he's a seasoned traveler. I only..." Paul began—but stopped.

"What dad?" Charlie looked over, seeing his father's silhouette outlined in the dark cab of the truck.

"Lots of mean people out there, son, and I hope he didn't meet up with someone who'd harm him."

Mean folks that did terrible things; not something Charlie thought a lot about. Laughter, shared meals, and countless acts of kindness filled their days, showcasing their deep family devotion. Nothing awful had touched his or his siblings except maybe a pet that got sick and crossed over.

Charlie stared into the night as the old truck rambled up the gravel drive toward the family farmhouse. His gaze went upward to the sky, dark, yet filled with stars that twinkled, and a three-quarter moon which hung effortlessly in the sky. With his window partially rolled down, the smells of dirt, hay, and cows drifted into his nostrils. His brows dipped. Was this the so-called dream life? He knew the Lewison house was brand-new construction, and grandiose; unlike their farmhouse, which creaked and moaned with every step on the wooden floors. Drafty and in some areas, cramped, and needing repairs, paint, or updating.

Why would that kid want to run off from that? Besides that, why would that boy want to run away from his momma? Charlie would never want to leave his family and run off. He'd been ticked off at his folks before, only never mad enough to run away. Gregg or Libby either; he loved his brother and sister and would miss them terribly.

Paul Koller killed the motor and undid his seat belt. "Come on, Charlie, let's get the feed out and into the barn. Your mom's probably wondering what took so long and I'm a betting our supper is cold."

"Yes, sir." Charlie followed suit and got out and met his dad at the tailgate of the truck to help unload the bags of feed.

He looked up into the sky and a shooting star
flashed by, then another. It was in that flash of a
moment that things could change for a person.

14

MIDNIGHT.

Harry Grist left to go to his ratty old short single-wide trailer at the edge of town. He had a half-acre lot, and before Arthur hired him, the man did odd jobs for town folk, and some seasonal work for the farmers or ranchers. Grist, a longtime resident of Hotspur, had fallen into tough times ten years back.

His parents were asleep. Or, as they liked to say, "they'd retired for the night." Such blowhard snobs. He sat atop his horse, lightly nudging him to move forward. The moon wasn't full, but there was enough light to see until he got to the back road and then he'd use his flashlight. He'd shoved a shovel handle with the head of the tool sticking out of the shotgun scabbard. Inside the saddlebags, he had a folded-up hoe in case he needed it.

As he rode, he thought about his mother and father. Why was he so different from them? If they were snobbish, why wasn't he? He figured being raised in this luxury of life, as they called it, he should have gained certain traits from them.

All the rich kids in the Bay Area he'd associated with were never fun; they held no interest in him; neither did the money; not like it should have, anyway.

He had envied Ryan Chapin's life. Poor and looked down on in the community, but they hadn't cared. Ryan's parents were involved in their children's everyday lives. They laughed, teased and without two nickels to rub together, the Chapin's had a happy family. Their food was basic, but it was food.

Their small house cramped, but it didn't matter to them. When he'd stayed the nights, he'd slept on an old cot with a worn-out sleeping bag and a flat pillow, and it was the best night's sleep ever. At home, he had a queen-sized bed with down-filled pillows and a duvet to cover him. A chef cooked his meals, and he never had to make a bed, clean up the dishes ... nothing. Any other kids would think this was heaven; Doug felt like he lived in hell.

It had been an accident the first time; but that's how it got started. The neighbor's cat had a litter of seven tiny fur balls. They hadn't wanted the kittens and were doling them out to whomever wanted one, and then getting their sweet, wayward momma cat fixed.

Ronald Jorgenson had offered a kitty to his mother, who declined. She was allergic. Doug was mad, real mad, and he didn't even know the reason. It was just a stupid cat. In secret, he snuck off and took one of the baby felines and hid it in his room.

After three days, his mother began sneezing and coughing. She complained he had to stop going next door to play with those animals because it was making her sick. A day later, she found cat hair on his bedding and went berserk.

Camille screamed, throwing a tantrum, and took Arthur's shaving strap and whipped Doug's bare behind, yelling at him that in the morning he would take that stupid cat back to the Jorgensen's and apologize.

Afterward, he would scrub all the cat hair out of his room and be thankful she didn't let his father discipline him.

As a ten-year-old boy, he had few ways to retaliate and took it out on the cat. He hadn't meant to, but once the limp body of the feline hung in his hands; he'd felt a strong sense of satisfaction and power. And thus, it began.

———

MARLIN WAS ASLEEP, WORN down from struggling to break free; and as soon as the hooves of the horse snapped and cracked twigs, his eyes popped open in pure fear.

Doug had returned.

At 14, he was smart enough to know this would be his last night as a breathing person. He'd prayed to a higher being and he hoped he'd been a decent enough person to gain entrance to heaven; because he was sure his abductor/killer was going to hell.

For Marlin Hudson, the night became the longest one he'd ever experienced before his soul left his earthly body; for Doug Lewison, it ended too fast, yet it satisfied him in ways that hadn't satisfied him since he had been that fifteen-year-old boy, dumping his first body in the Bay.

The pile of brush had been harder to manage digging under, and more work than he'd expected; only it was the cleverest spot to dispose of the body.

Funny how a kicking kid had been easier to manage than his lifeless body. How could this skin and bones kid be so heavy?

Doug rolled his eyes with a grin. "Dead weight," he said, his voice low, but giddy.

Thankful for wet earth underneath the dying brush pile, he could burrow further, and in a larger area. Broken limbs and bush yanked up out of the earth were easy to move and needed no hoeing or shoveling; and he'd had the fortune to have another brush pile near to borrow from. How'd anyone know if one pile shrunk a bit? It wasn't like old man Adair was out here measuring his piles of dead brush; and as far as Doug knew, the old guy was leaving them to decompose at nature's rate ... which could take years.

Exhausted, yet contented, Doug unsaddled his mount, did a quick brush down, and then shed his filthy, bloody clothes. Next, he took the red t-shirt, faded jeans, ratty tennis shoes, and holey socks the skinny youth had been wearing. He rolled them in a tight roll binding them with a thin strip of yellow nylon rope.

Dressed only in his underwear, Doug took the shovel and headed to the back side of the tack house.

With recent rains, the ground was soft enough and he dug a hole next to the structure, and under the bottom framing. At a sideways angle, he dug until he was under the tack house, then he shoved the rolled-up bundle in, packing down, covering the hole, tamping it more, and adding dirt.

Then he grabbed the water hose, soaked it, and added more dirt. Whatever he buried, he wanted it to stay buried.

He replaced the shovel and the hoe and went through the mud room up the back stairs to the first bathroom furthest from his parents' room; and took a long, hot shower.

The dirt, caked mud and blood swirled the drain, his sins washing away, he grinned.

By the time he'd showered and, dried, and got tucked away in his nice cozy bed, it was 4 am. Hired help Harry Grist would be here in two hours; most likely still fretting about that boy.

Too bad; he smiled as he drifted off to sleep.

15

THE YEAR 1986 BROUGHT fear into the smaller communities of Dove Crossing, Hotspur and River Run and an outer lying non-incorporated area called Link, Texas. This place was the pivotal point webbing out to connect the other three rural areas.

Picture an upside-down triangle: Hotspur top left, River Run top right, Dove Crossing at the bottom, with Link, Texas, in the middle. From there, you could drive to any of the three towns.

Link was a large, sparsely populated area with eleven homes: two unoccupied houses near the Auction Building, a one-room post office, a volunteer fire department with one old truck, and an EMT van serving the three nearby towns. Three residents grew cotton, two ran poultry farms, three families operated small market farms, one man ran the Auction Company, and a couple was adding ten RV stations to a new trailer park for ranchers hauling livestock to the Auction House.

If anyone thought River Run, Hotspur or Dove Crossing was small, Link, Texas, population 23, with two expectant mothers', might've been one of the top ten original BFE's.

The Auction Company ran cattle, farm equipment, and estate auctions; and even rented out for weddings, dances, and an occasional funeral. The Swisher family rented it one summer for a large family reunion, their first. It was at a family reunion a tragedy occurred, devastating the smaller town of Dove Crossing.

MOST OF THE SWISHERS were dairy farmers from Wisconsin and Iowa, in the business over ninety years and spread across the U.S. Sixty-one attended the reunion, including children, elders, newlyweds, and couples expecting their first or third child.

Day four of the Swisher Family Reunion.

The first of its kind, hosted by the Swisher Dairy Farm of Dove Crossing, Texas.

They used all ten RV hookups, and Pike Swisher had rented the two vacant houses for those without trailers; the homes also served as places to cook and store food and drinks.

The empty auction house was filled with charcoal grills, beer and Kool-Aid coolers, large water jugs, folding tables, and lawn chairs.

Outside, an uncle built a horseshoe pit and a washer-tossing area, while Pike had brought in ten dairy tubs so the kids could splash and play.

Groups sat chatting, playing cards or dominoes, and catching up on family gossip and jokes.

"Larry Jr. stop it, or Carla June, get out of that cooler, it's beer, or JIMMMMYYYY, where are you?" shouted out by moms and laughter peals persisted. Parents not at all worried about their children in such a remote

townless area, running free, and sometimes misbe-
having.

Teenagers got caught sipping a stolen bottle of beer
or wine from a box, and softly reprimanded, because
teens would be teens.

If any kid got green around the gills, the parent
knew they had smoked a stolen cigarette for the first
time—a lesson learned the hard way.

NIGHT FOUR WAS WINDING down, and tomorrow was Sunday.

It was the last day as everyone would start packing
up and getting the Auction House back in order, tidy-
ing the two rented houses, and general organization
for each party to leave and head home.

"Bekka, honey, where's Frannie, I haven't seen her in
a while?" Ron Swisher, a first cousin to Pike Swisher
by way of their fathers, asked his wife.

Bekka didn't look up as she gathered up three sets
of playing cards from the card table to separate. "She
asked if she could stay with Iris, uh, your second
cousin, Glenda's family in their RV tonight."

"Where's Luke off to?' Ron sat in the chair next to
his wife. Their eight-year-old son had been a handful
and Ron had been a smidge disappointed that he was
one of the boys who'd broken a window on one of the
houses Pike leased for the long weekend. Ron, Troy,
and Gus all gave Pike money for the repairs, because
it was their three boys who caused the breakage.

"He's with Troy's boy, Matt. I said he could stay the
night with them, I thought it'd be okay, give us a night

alone," she patted her growing belly, "until this little one makes his or her appearance." Bekka let out a deep sigh, pulling over a chair to sit. "Hard to stand on my feet too long these days."

Ron massaged his wife's shoulders. "Let's get an early start tomorrow, we might be the first to leave, and you being seven months pregnant, no one will get mad."

Seven months pregnant with a surprise baby at their age; her forty-one and Ron forty-eight; another baby seemed ludicrous, but here they were, expecting again.

Their daughter, Frannie, hated farm life, though she never complained. She was usually subdued and sad. Her joy came from school, summer camps, band, and church, but as a fifteen-year-old, she longed for a best friend—and in her fourth-removed cousin Iris, she had found one. The two had spent the past two days having a blast, promising to write and call. Iris even suggested they could plan next summer to spend the first half in Iron River and the second half in Terre Haute, Indiana—and the girls had already worked out the plan.

"Frannie's had such a grand time, Ron, I'm so glad we came." His wife smiled at him, and he smiled back.

"Iris' family are decent people, and I trust that side of my mom's family, even though they don't farm," Ron said jokingly.

———

"OKAY, IRIS, I'LL TAP on the back side of the trailer, and you come let me in, I promise to be back here by eleven."

"Are you sure, Frannie, what if you get caught, or what if he, well, you know?"

"He won't, he's not that kinda guy, I can tell. And it's just one last night, anyway. Besides, he lives in Colorado, and I'll never see him again, this is just a summer fling."

"Summer fling, right, how about a weeklong fling at most?" Iris burst into laughter.

Frannie shrugged, and said, "And with a what, fifth removed cousin of a great aunt or uncle I never knew existed? I just want to say goodbye, and kiss him a few more times, because, well, it's been yummy, and then I can go home and brag to," she scrunched up her nose, "no one in my tiny town!"

"I get it, tiny town, no boys, no romance for you. When you come to Terre Haute, we are going to have a blast; and girl, there are enough cute boys to go around. Shoot, you might even fall in love and move in with us!"

"Yeah, well, my mom having another baby will curb that from happening. And I'd miss my family. But can't wait for a mini vacation away from them."

The girls hugged, and Frannie ran off to find Heath, the shy, cute fifth-removed cousin on her father's mother's side. Keeping track of who was whose cousin—and whether by blood or marriage—was a headache. Frannie was glad Heath was a cousin by marriage; it made things a lot less awkward.

16

"I CAN'T BELIEVE WE are leaving tomorrow. Seems like I just met you." He draped his arm over her shoulder as they strolled away from the rear of the building, toward the cattle stalls and the barn.

The teens had found that the area behind the barn was the best make-out spot. Younger kids steered clear because somebody had started a ghost story about a witch roaming the backwoods.

"Oh, my lord, we did just meet you, goofball," Frannie snickered. Heath was cute and could kiss, though he was a year younger and a bit of a doofus. The attraction between them had been strong.

Frannie had never had a fella, and it wasn't just because she lived in a tiny town. She'd lost twenty pounds, still had another fifteen to go, and had started wearing a little makeup and styling her hair. On a dairy farm that churned out creamy cheeses, butters, ice cream, and ice-cold milk, she hadn't cared about her weight until she hit thirteen.

"This has been the best time, Frannie. Thanks for letting me kiss you."

"Heath! Lord! You don't have to say that, especially if I'm okay with it and like it." Frannie leaned in, and in three seconds they were wrapped up like two fishing worms.

After the kiss, they walked to a huge fallen tree. Sitting on the ground, leaning against it, they chatted under the starry night—kissing, holding hands, and talking about love, and how they hoped they each found it once.

Heath stood, and Frannie frowned at her backlit digital Casio watch. "It's only nine-thirty. You in a hurry to leave me?"

"No, I gotta go pee."

Frannie blushed. "Oh, yeah. Sure." Discussing bodily functions at her age was, well, gross.

IN THE BACK AREA, eyes watched the teens. They just kissed and talked—not much excitement. The girl was nice-looking, a little chubby, with a pretty face and a forward attitude.

The observer had seen several sets of teens and pre-teens filter through this area—kissing and even some over-the-clothes heavy petting.

After hearing about the huge family reunion from Dove Crossing's cheering squad grapevine, he wanted to see for himself. That many people related in one place looked like a small village. What amazed him were the kissing cousins, and how some took it a few steps further. Teenage hormones were running full speed this weekend—including his.

He knew this was the last night of the reunion. He hoped for the short-haired brunette and the tall, gangly fella they called Skip. Her name was Beth, and she was a hellcat. She had practically devoured Skip, scaring him and slowing him down—much to Doug's frustration that first night. After that, he hadn't seen them again.

The few other couples he saw were just kids goofing around, none with sexual experience—not that he had any himself, though he knew more.

"Took you long enough. You get lost or what?" Frannie huffed when Heath sat down.

"No, I'm just... not feeling so good." He hurried off and Frannie heard him upchuck. Gross!

Wiping his mouth with the back of his hand, he cleared his throat. "Sorry, Fran. I gotta get water and lie down. I think that stew was too spicy." He held out a hand. "Come on, let's get back."

"No, you go on, Heath. I'll sit here, enjoy the silence, the stars, and think."

"By yourself? Frannie, come on."

A laugh bubbled. "Heath Cartright, are you scared? Did the make-believe ghost story get to you?"

He frowned. "No, but I believe in coyotes and stuff. It ain't safe out here alone, with no protection."

"And you were planning to protect me by what—carrying me on your shoulders and running?"

"Francine Swisher, that's not very nice. I'd do more than run—I'd die before letting a coyote get to you."

As if on cue, the distant howls of a coyote pack sounded.

"Well, dork, we have wild animals on our farm. Some could be bears—much worse than a coyote. Look, I'm a big girl," she dared, eyes challenging him. "I'm a fair runner, even with a little flab. Go ahead. You've already ruined the night by yakking. Besides, we're not in love. This was just a stupid weeklong fling." She jerked her head back, letting her mousy blonde hair swing.

Pissed off, Heath waved. "It was a pleasure to meet you—fifth cousin removed, not by blood. Maybe we'll see each other at the next reunion I won't attend." He stomped off. She flipped him off in the dark, leaned into the fallen tree trunk, closed her eyes, and thought, *boys!*

———

SHE WASN'T SURE HOW long she sat there when a hand reached from behind and covered her eyes. Her first thought was Heath.

"Oh, ha-ha-ha. Heath, are you trying to scare me? Feeling better and want some more kisses?"

The deeper voice made her spine stiffen, her heart rate increasing.

"I'm not that stupid boy; you deserve someone who can appreciate you."

She didn't bolt. Under his touch, he felt her forehead furrow as she struggled to recognize the voice. Was it another family member?

"Is that you, Will, you little weasel?"

"Nope. Not Will. Better."

Confused and scared, she thought maybe an older man had taken a liking to her. She tried to rise, but his hands held her shoulders down. Her body tensed. He grinned and lifted the roll of duct tape, pressing it over her mouth so she could not scream, then turned her to face him.

She saw he was not part of the reunion. Where had he come from?

———

GONE. FRANNIE—NOWHERE TO BE found. Bekka and Ron were frantic.

Glenda consoled a sobbing Iris. Frannie and Heath had been meeting for a "kissing date" and had never shown up at their RV.

"I... I fell asleep, and... Frannie never knocked on the back of the RV," Iris sobbed.

"Glenda, did you know she wanted to go there?" Ron raked a hand through his wild hair, voice terse.

"No, I mean, Iris said Frannie was coming over in an hour. Me and Dave went to our sleeping quarters, so I just figured she'd show up later. I didn't check; didn't feel there was a need."

Bekka laid a hand on Ron's arm. "It's not Glenda's fault, and she had no reason to worry. We should search for her, out there." Her gaze cut toward the woods. "She might be lost or hurt."

———

NO FRANNIE—JUST A SHOE. The clan felt heartbroken, suspecting she was gone... forever.

The towns—Hotspur, Dove Crossing, and River Run—organized a search. The Sheriff and State Police got involved in the man-girl hunt.

After the largest grid search the area had ever seen, they had not found her. Life had to move forward for the Swisher family, returning home with prayers that she would be found.

The lack of a corpse ruled out wild animals. A drifter passing through seemed the only explanation.

Bekka emphatically denied that Frannie would run away. She was happy with her new friend, Iris, and had been planning next summer's visit. "No, our daughter is not a runaway."

RON RELUCTANTLY TOOK HIS pregnant wife and son home to Iron River, Wisconsin, without Frannie. Authorities promised to continue searching and keep them up-dated.

Camille Lewison felt a stirring in her heart—a fright-ening stir. Doug's reaction to the missing girl worried her. He had taken to leaving the house late at night all week.

When she asked where he went, he always said, "Just for a drive, to get out of the house." His excuse was no friends, and why should she care? If she cared, they'd move back to California. He stomped off, slamming the door in anger.

Art was passive—not caring if the child was there or not. Her husband had never wanted to be a father; this role had been foisted upon him.

Camille's fear of Doug grew daily. She knew she had to act, but what could she do? She blamed herself for not locking him up when the first girl died... she was sure Doug had killed her, just like the kittens.

AFTER THE EVENT, LOCAL law enforcement monitored vagrants, vetting and detaining them. Few people crossed the area, and it took a while for spirits to lift and fear to dissipate. Yet, time marched on.

17

After the event, local law enforcement monitored veterans' venting and detaining if any. Few people crossed the line, and it took a wife for spirits to lift and rest to disappear yet time and again.

1987–1988

It was their sophomore year.

Eighth and ninth grades went by in a flash—the lines between the years blurred, yet the memories remained vivid and cherished. Adolescent characteristics gave way to the mannerisms of young adults. Although many displayed adult-like behavior, sometimes their youthfulness peeked through.

A few years ago, Charlie and his pals were underage drivers, only allowed to drive on their own land or county roads, avoiding the blacktop streets. But getting those small plastic licenses—wow, what a game changer!

Sixteen with a driver's license meant ranch and farm boys could finally head into town on the blacktop, without fear of a ticket. It helped when parents needed supplies, locally or in Junction or River Run.

The real game changer was socializing—and privacy in a two-door or four-door dating machine. The kicker: having the nerve to ask a girl out, and praying she'd say yes.

Boys.

They matured slower than girls.

First kisses, handholding, a dab of other hanky-panky had already happened, but most small-town teens acted moral and wholesome.

Some didn't; they had their own singular clique.

Smart kids, or sports jocks who played every sport—not just one—because there weren't enough boys for all the separate teams.

Football was thrilling.

Small towns played six-man, and Tara Swanson still laughed about the night Neal caught his first touchdown pass. He ran so far past the goal post, they thought they'd need a floodlight to find him.

Country boys had agility and talent to match.

If they weren't tall, they made effective guards in basketball.

Skinny and fast? The coach, also the math teacher, placed them as wide receivers or running backs.

All schools had bullies.

Small towns had a few, but they were stopped by those defending the weaker, less popular, or poorer students.

Most country kids had zero tolerance. Doug Lewison learned that quickly.

Pretty girls tried out for cheerleading, and the boys voted yea or nay. They cheered at all sporting events—except the ones they participated in.

Most cheerleaders were also on the girls' basketball team. Fifth graders to seniors took part in the twirling squad. The uniforms were handmade by older ladies, avid quilters, who contributed their sewing skills. Skirts, pompoms, and shoe poms were passed down from graduating or "retired" ex-cheerleaders.

Clubs like 4-H (Head-Heart-Hands-Health) and Future Farmers of America welcomed both boys and girls, offering hands-on experience with livestock and farming.

Then came the glorious rodeo days.

Bull riding, calf roping, prize heifers or pigs, maybe a sheep.

Jam-making, pie-baking, or quilting contests.

Blue ribbons and family fun.

The rodeo was an adventure, a road trip to Kerrville, Texas.

Twelve days of horse, cow, and pig manure—and some years, sheep dung.

Cowboys in chaps, boots, and spurs. Girls with hair in pigtails under cowboy hats, boots on their feet.

Wholesome activities that drew the entire town, stores closed so everyone could watch local boys ride bulls, bust broncos, and rope calves while girls competed in barrel racing.

Rodeo memories.

Lyssa Caldwell had hers.

In the fall of 1987, Lyssa, Kadie Hopkins, Tara Swanson, and Cathy Nunez, the new girl, walked behind the horse barns, chatting, admiring livestock and boys from surrounding schools.

"Look, there's that creep, Doug," Lyssa said, cutting her eyes toward the paddock.

"I think he's cute, don't y'all?" Cathy sneaked a peek.

"He might be, but he's weird. Cathy, you're new—best stay away from him," Tara advised.

"Does he have a girlfriend?" Cathy's voice lowered. "Maybe he just needs the right one."

"No. None of the girls at Hotspur likes him," Kadie said, turning her back. "There's something off. Be careful around him."

"Oh, you guys, y'all just want to scare me. Doug's just a regular guy—with a lot of money," Cathy snickered.

"Let's check which sheep won the blue ribbon," Lyssa said, walking away from the corral.

An hour later, at the paddock entrance, the girls had forgotten about Doug—until he appeared on horseback.

"Ladies, you all look very nice tonight."

Kadie piped up, "What do you want, Doug?"

"You don't have to be nasty, Miss Prom Queen," Doug said, his face crinkling, then softening as he looked at Cathy. "Hi Cathy. Didn't you move here from... Midland or Odessa?"

"Neither. Wickett—a tiny, poor town."

"I didn't know that. So where did you go to school?" Lyssa asked.

"All the kids from Pyote and Wickett went to Monahans."

Doug's insides jerked. Had she known Marlin Hudson?

"Hey Cathy, want to go for a horseback ride with me?"

Kadie touched Cathy's arm to warn her off, but Cathy smiled. "Sure."

Doug lifted her behind him, glanced at the other girls. "I'll have her back before midnight." He spurred the horses, trotting off, with Kadie calling, "Meet us at the concession stand afterward." Cathy gave a thumbs-up.

CATHY CHANGED AFTER THAT night—and not for the better.

Although a romantic relationship blossomed between her and Doug, unsettling tension grew.

She had laughed and been pleasant, but now she was dark and sullen. If Doug saw her talking to another boy, he clung to her, a buffer between them and anyone else.

In the ladies' bathroom, Lyssa cornered her.

"Are you okay, Cath?"

"I'm fine," Cathy replied, not looking at her.

"Cathy, no you're not. Break up with him—he has you tied in knots, scared of your own shadow."

Audra Rafferty emerged from a stall. "Lyssa's right. Isn't he leaving for college after graduation?"

"Yeah, but he wants me to come to San Antonio, finish school there, live with him, and have my college paid for."

"Your mom? Has she met him?"

"She doesn't like him."

"Smart woman," Audra said. "You haven't been yourself since that moonlight horseback ride. I want that sweet girl back."

She left Lyssa and Cathy alone.

———

CATHY, A FRESHMAN, WAS a year younger than Lyssa and three years younger than Audra and Kadie. Traveling to San Antonio with Doug Lewison seemed unwise.

Lyssa and Audra feared Doug was exploiting Cathy's family's poverty. Not destitute, but hand-to-mouth. Cathy's father was unemployed, her mother did odd jobs. Her older brother worked at the Swisher dairy to help support them.

Her friends had provided the money for school outings; Doug had money and showered her with gifts when he felt it necessary. Money—a powerful pull.

After that horseback ride, Cathy thought she'd found love. What she found was a terrifying monster she planned to milk for cash as long as she could endure his abuse. It seemed her only way out of poverty and streets at a young age.

18

THE NIGHTTIME SKY WAS cloudless and crisp, the air cool with a slight hint of wind.

The grassy football field was open, with wooden bleachers on either side and plenty of folks in folding lawn chairs, lightweight blankets wrapped around their shoulders.

Kids ran and played in and around the bleachers while parents geared up for the game.

An announcer called out each team as they ran from the locker room onto the field, the small crowd hollering!

Both teams, with their coaches and assistants, stood in front of the empty metal benches along the side of the field between the 25- and 50-yard lines.

Suited up in pads, cleats, and helmets, each boy was eager to play. Before the game started, they played the Star-Spangled Banner; everyone stood, hands on hearts, hats off, singing with pride.

Kickoff!

A fast-paced game with six-man teams on real grass and dirt—the best kind of game. And oh, the games in rain, with mud and muck, slipping and sliding—sheer joy in the elements Mother Nature delivered. These were the memories each player recalled in their heyday.

Hotspur's Hawks came out strong, scoring a touchdown by the end of the first quarter, but they missed the extra point.

It stayed 6–0 until the third quarter, when the Caster High Crows scored a touchdown—and made their extra point.

At fourth down, Hotspurs QB Tye Slater passed to Gregg Koller, who ran it in for another touchdown; but Evan Dyer missed the extra point.

The score was now 7–12 going into the fourth quarter.

Cowbells clanged as the cheerleaders led the crowd in the famous cheer: "We got spirit, yes we do! We got spirit, how about you?"

Across the field, the opposing crowd screeched it back, growing louder each time until the cheer faded.

The cheerleaders—Katie Hopkins, Lyssa Caldwell, Brinna Neeson, Patty Goodwin, and Tara Swanson—formed a V and did the "Victory" cheer.

Once the cheer was over, they turned to watch the game—all except Lyssa, who scanned the crowd for Cathy Nunez.

She'd seen Cathy earlier sitting with the slimeball Doug, but they weren't in the stands anymore.

Doug wasn't into sports; he didn't even like the game. Cathy had talked him into joining school functions at least once. He'd been pressuring her to decide about moving to San Antonio with him, and she had hemmed and hawed, unwilling to give a definite answer.

Lyssa moved next to Kadie and asked, "Hey, where did Cathy and Doug get off to?"

Kadie, focused on her new beau Tye Slater, swayed her head. "Don't know."

Lyssa moved to the end behind the others, scanning the area. She didn't see Cathy at the concession stand or near the school building. Mr. and Mrs. Nunez sat in the third row; she waved, then turned to Brinna Neeson. "Hey, Brin, I'm going to the restroom. Be back in a jiff."

"Well hurry, the game's almost over, and it looks like we'll win!"

Lyssa nodded and ran, hoping to spot Cathy along the way.

With less than a minute left, the Hawks intercepted the ball on the twenty-yard line; the crowd counted down the clock in a frenzy.

The whistle blew. The game ended. The Hotspurs crowd cheered, jumping up and down, hugging.

Kadie ran onto the grassy field, cool earth beneath her feet, throwing her arms around quarterback Tye Slater. Evan, Charlie, and their teammates celebrated with chest bumps and high fives.

Patty and Brinna tossed their pom-poms, screamed, and hugged. Both teams showed proper sportsmanship; coaches shook hands, and players lined up to say "good game" before heading to the locker rooms.

Lyssa grabbed her cheering gear and trotted to her mom and little brother. "Mom, can you hold on to these for me?"

"Honey, we need to go. Danny's tired, and I have an early day tomorrow."

"Mom, I need to find Cathy. I'm worried about her."

"You think you can get a friend to take you home? I need to get this kid to bed." Doris Caldwell gave her a pleading look.

"I can get a ride. Don't worry about me. Get Danny home."

"Lyssa, you sure?"

"Wait here, I'll be right back." Lyssa sprinted toward Kadie and Tye, stood for a second, then ran back. "Kadie and Tye will drive me home."

"Alright, see you soon. Don't stay out late," Doris said, hoisting Danny to his feet. "Come on, son, let's get you home and in bed."

"Here, Mom, I'll carry the pom-poms, bag, and blanket. You get Danny."

At the car, Lyssa gave her mom a swift peck on the cheek. "I'll be home soon, I promise." She darted off to look for Cathy, not caring if Doug stayed behind. A sense of dread filled her stomach.

No one had seen Cathy or Doug leave. Mrs. Nunez was still there. Lyssa stopped her.

"Did Cathy leave?"

The older woman shrugged. "If she did, she didn't tell me. Lyssa, she's not been coming home at night. Do you know where she's been going? My daughter doesn't talk to me anymore."

"I'm sorry, Mrs. Nunez, she didn't tell me anything." Lyssa's heart sank. Cathy had been staying with Doug. It was the only answer.

"If you see her, will you ask her to please come home?"

"Yes, ma'am, I will." Lyssa promised.

The older lady walked off, and Lyssa saw the worry in her eyes.

"Hi, Lyssa, terrific game, huh?" Charlie said, stopping.

"Yeah, you guys played better tonight than ever. Hey, did you see Cathy and Doug?"

Charlie frowned. "Nope, not since halftime. I don't like the guy; he's a scary weirdo. And why does your friend like him? No one understands it."

"Can't answer that. Doug's a mean creep."

"Lyssa, Tye and I are ready to leave. You coming?"

"Oh, I... well, I guess I have no choice."

"Need a ride home? I can give you a lift," Charlie offered.

She bit her bottom lip. Two years ago, they had a summer puppy love fling. Then it just ended—no fight, no reason.

Lyssa looked at Kadie with the "you think I should?" look.

"Since you live on the way to the Kollers, let Charlie take you. Tye won't have to double-back."

Kadie knew how Lyssa felt about Charlie. She still had feelings for him. She'd liked him even while dating Wendall from Dove Crossing. They'd dated almost ten months before she found out he had an out-of-town girlfriend. Wendall Oats had another girl in Dove Crossing too.

Charlie's dating life was different.

He'd had a handful of casual dates—maybe a movie, a school dance—nothing steady. His time went to working the ranch with his dad and brother; hunting deer and quail in fall, wild boar in spring, bagging turkeys if lucky. Baseball and football practice kept him busy. He barely had time to breathe, let alone date.

He looked at Lyssa, still the most beautiful of all Hotspurs' girls, and his heart zinged.

Charles Allen Koller was ready for a girl in his life; he needed to make time.

Lyssa was smart, athletic, wholesome. Their freshman year, he'd pushed her aside for ranch work, but maybe she'd enjoy hunting or outdoorsy things—he'd never asked.

Charlie felt like kicking himself for not giving it a try. Small town, deep love. That night, they rekindled a relationship—one meant to be from the start.

"Alright, Charlie, I'd be thankful for a ride home." Lyssa said, turning to Kadie. "See you in the morning, front of the cafeteria, okay?"

"I will. Be careful." Kadie gave a sad smile, then left with Tye.

"Be careful? What'd Kadie mean?" Charlie asked, brow creased.

"Oh," she said, nerves taut, "not you, Charlie. I'm worried about Cathy."

"I know Doug's a mean guy, but he wouldn't hurt her, right? I've never seen any signs of abuse."

"Well, no, not physical. But I think he's the psychological-abusing type. Just some things Cathy told me. I don't want to break her confidence, understand?"

Charlie stepped closer, taking her hand in his, lacing their fingers.

"Lyssa, you can trust me with anything, I swear." His look melted her heart. She relaxed, letting her hand fit into his, and squeezed.

"They've been... uh, best way to say it is 'doing it.' She told me he's rough and makes her do stuff I don't want to repeat." Charlie watched her shudder.

"Then let's go look for her."

"Charlie, if she's at his house, we can't just barge in."

"Let's go into town, see if he took her home, then check the Lewisons'—see if Doug's car is there. That's all we can do tonight; too late to knock on doors."

She nodded. "You're right. Sorry I'm such a worry-wart. I just have an awful feeling."

Charlie remembered when Marlin Hudson ran off, how wrong it felt. He'd only met the child once when Mr. Grist and Marlin were at JJ's Dry Goods. They acted more like father and son than old man and run-away—so the teen leaving hadn't felt right.

But he was only twelve then.

What did he know back then about runaways?

He had a happy home life with no worries about his next meal or a roof over his head.

19

THE NIGHT OF THE winning football game, they hadn't found Cathy—at least they didn't see her. Doug's car was parked in the long driveway, and the Nunez family still hadn't heard from their eldest daughter.

Neither Cathy nor Doug showed up at school the next day. Questions piled up, with no answers as to where Cathy had gone.

Lyssa called the Nunez home. "Is Cathy home?"

"Is this Lyssa?" Mrs. Nunez's voice was small.

"Yes, ma'am."

"No, she never came home. Has she been at school?"

"No, she hasn't. I'm very concerned about her."

"Her father and I are worried sick. Can you find out if she's at that boy's house?"

"I... okay. My friend and I will drive over and see what we can find. If you hear from her, will you let me know?"

"Lyssa, please, call me after you go to that boy's house, will you? Reynoldo is ready to drag her by the hair and beat the daylights out of that boy. I'm scared; I don't want my son in prison." Mrs. Nunez burst into tears.

"Tell him to wait until Charlie and I go look for her and speak with the Lewisons, please."

"Yes, yes, call me soon." The older woman hung up, then sat in the nearest chair, sobbing with shaking hands.

The phone rang again. She snatched it up.

"Momma?"

"Cathy, oh Cathy, come home, mija (darling), please."

"Listen, Mom, I need to tell you something, and please don't cry," Cathy said, her tone low and nervous, explaining her plans.

"No, no! Do not sell yourself to him, Cathy! You aren't that kind of person," Mrs. Nunez pleaded. But Cathy didn't listen. She whispered a goodbye and disconnected.

Mrs. Nunez sat stunned, unable to believe her daughter was leaving the family because the boy was paying her to go with him. Cathy had promised her mother the money would help the family, and she believed this was her only way.

Now, Mrs. Nunez had to break the news to Roberto, Cathy's father, and restrain Reynaldo from taking violent action against Doug. It was a hard conversation. Raw emotions in the Nunez household hung heavy, like a death shroud.

Deep inside, a dread filled Mrs. Nunez's heart. Her daughter was gone—not briefly, but forever. She would never see her alive again. The words formed in her brain and dropped with a resounding thud into her heart.

As promised, Lyssa called back. That's when she learned Cathy had phoned her mother to say she was leaving Hotspur and moving to San Antonio with Doug. From their quick visit to the Lewisons, Lyssa and

Charlie discovered Doug had packed and left, without saying goodbye—no note, nothing.

Lyssa and Charlie stood on the front porch of the massive house with the Lewisons.

"I cannot believe he'd just up and take off. He won't even be here for his senior graduation," Camille fretted.

"That boy," Arthur Lewison said, tightening his lips.

Harry Grist's truck threw gravel as he drove up, parked, and got out. He waved a jerk of his head at the foursome. "Morning. Everything alright?"

A brief rundown brought Grist up to date.

"He's a grown man. Guess he made his choice, huh?" Harry Grist wasn't sad. He didn't care for their son and didn't trust him. He suspected him of harming Marlin, but there was no proof.

He felt bad for the girl, but kept it to himself. If Cathy were smart and lucky, she'd escape Doug and never see him again—but Grist suspected it was too late.

The school mailed Doug's diploma to his parents that spring. With Cathy gone, Mrs. Nunez sank into a deep depression and took her own life. She left behind an ill husband, two younger children, and her eldest son Reynaldo. Twenty-two-year-old Rey found himself responsible for caring for the family.

After her death, Reynaldo packed up his family and returned to Wickett, Texas. A friend's father offered to teach him the mechanics trade, what he felt was best for his family.

The ordeal left Lyssa heartbroken, enraged at Cathy for tearing her family apart, and filled with an intense hatred for Doug Lewison.

Girls at school whispered that Cathy might be pregnant, and that this was a way to hide her shame. Had

Doug taken her to the big city for an abortion? In a few months, they might return with a concocted story of homesickness.

What a miserable homecoming that would be: Cathy's mother dead, her family gone, no home. Lyssa and her mom agreed that if Cathy ever returned, she could live with them.

Lyssa's tender heart and thoughtful actions made Charlie fall even more in love with her.

Doug Lewison could stay away forever—they all hoped he would. Everyone but his parents, who had mixed feelings about their son.

Camille unlocked a box of medical records and spread them across the eight-foot dining room table: reports on her sister Lucinda's health. Diagnosed at ten with manic-depressive disorder and at fourteen with schizophrenia, Lucinda's paranoia had been so severe her parents institutionalized her until she was seventeen. Therapy and medication helped. On her eighteenth birthday, she returned home, nearly normal. Then came Gordon Drake: dashing, fun-loving, daring, a college boy from an upper-class upbringing. Lucinda fell hard.

After their first wedding anniversary, Lucinda confided in Camille that Gordon was bipolar and on medication. Camille felt as if an elephant sat on her chest when Lucinda revealed she was pregnant. With her schizophrenia, disconnections from reality, paranoia, and delusions, Camille worried. Gordon's bipolar diagnosis compounded her concern.

They both wondered how medications and genetics would affect the child. Camille researched and found that while the child's risk was higher, it wasn't certain. Environmental factors and home life could reduce the risk. This eased Camille somewhat, but she still worried. How loving would Lucinda and Gordon be? Camille never imagined she'd become a mother figure to her sister's child.

An hour later, Arthur found Camille with her head on the table, pages wadded and in disarray.

"Camille?" He touched her shoulder; she jumped.

"Oh, Art, what have we done?"

"What do you mean, dear?"

"That boy... he is part Gordon and part Lucinda. And we knew."

Arthur pulled out a chair. "What is it you think we knew?"

"We knew it was him that killed those kittens and other pets back in California. Now Cathy... and that other girl..."

He shushed her. "No proof, Camille. Not an ounce."

Tears welled in her tired eyes. "Yes, there was."

"No, honey. The police found nothing connecting him."

She slid her hand to a stack of Instamatic photos: dead animals and one young woman. "They were in Doug's room."

"Camille, my god, officials could implicate us in a cover-up if anyone ever saw these." Arthur rose, grabbing the photos, but Camille stopped him.

"Art. Stop. Go talk to Grist. I'll clear this up. Don't fret." Her voice was calm, her demeanor unhurried.

He exhaled shakily. "I just can't believe you didn't say something. Why, Camille?"

"And lose the only child I'll ever have? No, dear. I had to protect my son. Now go. Leave me to clear this away."

Without another word, Arthur Lewison walked out through the dining room, past the kitchen, and to the mudroom. His heart raced; his troubled past flashed before him.

Camille heard the back door shut, gathered the papers, and stacked them to replace them in the wall safe.

She would do anything to keep her son safe.

20

In mid-May 1988, two weeks after Gregg's graduation, the family had a teary farewell; he was off to boot camp after making the crucial decision to join the Army.

"Look, Dad," Gregg said, "no scholarship, and I won't have you and Mom going into debt for tuition money. Join the Army, get a degree—that's my plan."

He turned to Charlie. "You, little brother, go after that scholarship—baseball or your brains. Got it?"

With a crooked, sad smile, Charlie saluted. "Yes, sir!"

Poor Libby. She'd boo-hooed over Gregg leaving harder than their mother had.

"Greggy, don't get shot, please!" she clung to his leg.

"Aw, come on, Lib. It ain't war—it's only training camp." Gregg ruffled her hair and hugged her.

"All right, we gotta let Gregg get going. Don't want him to be late, do we?" Paul Koller said, emotion thick in his throat. One down, two kids left to leave the nest; this was the saddest thought Lindy and Paul could imagine.

With his gear packed, Gregg climbed into the driver's seat of his thirteen-year-old Camaro, a car born to be a classic. He pulled away as they waved until all they saw was white dust and a dot of his midnight-blue car in the distance.

Gregg's chosen military path was Army Medic. His work on the ranch and caring for cattle had sparked an interest in medicine, and his grades in science, biology, and anatomy were above average. Hotspur High, a One-A school, hadn't offered chemistry or physiology, so Gregg studied everything he could find at the Junction library.

By August 1990, the Gulf War put tremendous stress on the family. Whenever possible, they stayed glued to CNN. February 1991 brought relief—not just to the Kollers, but to the nation—as Operation Desert Shield–Desert Storm ended.

SEASONS CHANGED, EVENTS UNFOLDED, and time marched forward. Years passed in the blink of an eye, bringing noticeable changes to the town: new shops, wider roads, and modern conveniences such as gas stations, doctors' offices, and larger grocery stores, with the possibility of chain stores.

With newcomers moving in, the rural feel began to fade. Daily routines and long-held traditions were affected. Graduations sent Hotspur kids off to college or jobs in larger towns. Marriages and new babies arrived, and older ranchers and farmers prepared for retirement, selling tracts of land.

"MOMMA!" LIBBY BOUNDED INTO the house, muddy boots and all. Wide-eyed, Lindy Koller pointed.

"Get back into the mudroom, young lady! Shuck those boots, and for heaven's sake, wash your hands! Heaven help me, you're far worse than either of your brothers were."

"Yeah, I know. I'm a disgrace to girls all over the world. Listen, Mom, Mr. Glen says he's planning on selling some land."

Lindy looked at her daughter. "Are you thinking about buying it?" She pinched her lips together.

"Well, ha-ha-ha, Mom, you're hilarious. And if I could, yes, I would. But it's the land he owns way south of town—not next door to us."

"Who on earth would want that piece of land? It's not good for planting or grazing."

Libby grabbed an apple from the counter and bit into it, chewing thoughtfully. "Some company—uh, Drees... oh, yeah, Del Mar Homes Builders. They're going to build tract homes, or a master-planned community or something like that."

"Well," Lindy said, "guess that means our town is going to grow some."

"Yeah, maybe they'll build us a Piggly Wiggly or an HEB, so we don't have to drive so far for groceries."

Lindy smiled. "That would be nice, now, wouldn't it?"

Town growth was inevitable. Some small towns were never destined to expand, but as tiny towns grew, city limits blurred.

HARRY GRIST THOUGHT OF Marlin Hudson often. He would now be about twenty—not a boy, but a man. Grist was confident Marlin had found his father and hoped that one day he'd hear from him. Never having married or had a child of his own, Marlin had filled that tiny gap for a while. Harry never expected Marlin's departure to create such a void in his heart.

Cathy Nunez would be seventeen. Lyssa prayed wherever she was that Cathy had stayed in school and was happy. Every day she was gone, Lyssa hoped for a call, a letter, even a postcard—but nothing came.

Several times over the years, she'd dropped by the Lewison home, hoping for news, but Doug never called or visited. Camille became withdrawn, a shut-in. Arthur attended a few town functions alone, his gaunt face and tired eyes betraying the toll Doug's disappearance had taken.

Today would be Lyssa's last attempt to reach out—at least one more time. Borrowing her mom's car, she drove to the now run-down house on the hill. In just four years, the grand home the Lewisons had built on the front five acres had become worn and neglected. Word had spread that Arthur sold off his small herd of fifty cattle, keeping only a few mangy sheep and a couple of goats. Mr. Grist stayed on to help, but there wasn't much left to maintain.

They welcomed her into the front sitting room. Camille lay covered with a blanket on the chaise lounge. Lyssa started at how frail the woman looked—jaundiced skin, sunken cheeks.

"Water or a soda?" Arthur asked, a gracious host.

"No thank you, Mr. Lewison. I just came by to ask if you'd heard from your son."

"No, I'm sorry, young lady, but he hasn't called—not once. Not even for money, which isn't like him at all."

"Have you and Mrs. Lewison considered calling the police in San Antonio? Maybe they can check into something?" Lyssa grasped at straws.

"We did, but Doug isn't a minor. He has free will; they won't do anything. We've considered hiring a private investigator—but we don't even know where to start. What about that girl's dad or brother? Heard anything?" Arthur asked, knowing about Mrs. Nunez's suicide but not keeping up with the rest of Cathy's family.

"No, sir. Not a peep," Lyssa said, defeated.

A soft voice sounded from the chaise. "He ain't ever coming back. He's gone—for good." Camille closed her eyes.

"Shush, honey." Arthur glanced at Lyssa, motioning her to follow him into another room. "My wife is ill, and I'd rather not upset her."

"I know this has been difficult for her. Losing your son must've been devastating."

"Let me escort you to the door, and thank you for checking in. It's been nice of you to care. You're the only one from Hotspur who gave a damn—well, you and Harry Grist. Ever since that woman hanged herself, the town shunned us." Fire ignited in his next words. "You'd think we'd been the ones who put the noose around Mrs. Nunez's neck."

"Small-town mentality, I'm sorry, Mr. Lewison. By the way, I saw a bulldozer and an excavator behind your property. Are you rebuilding?"

"No, young lady. Demolishing. Since we're not running cattle, and sold the other livestock—including the horses—we don't need the tack building or barn. After clearing the land, Camille and I plan to move back to California. I have family there."

"Are you selling the house, then?"

"I suppose the developers can turn it into a main office if they want."

"Land developers are buying you out?"

His leathery face creased in a grin. "No, we're selling out. This place holds terrible memories for Camille. With Doug gone, she wants to spend her golden years on the West Coast."

"How long before you leave? And what if Doug comes home?"

"Maybe within the year. And honey, he ain't coming home. I can tell you why I know that."

Lyssa frowned. "You can?"

"Doug hasn't touched the bank account we set up for him in three years, and he's been gone four. This can only mean one thing—my son is dead." Art's tone was flat, matter-of-fact. "Let me walk you to the door, Ms. Caldwell."

Lyssa sat in her mom's 1980 Ford Taurus, seatbelt fastened, but didn't start the car. Her eyes drifted toward the house and the land beyond. Doug—dead? If so, where was Cathy? Could Mr. and Mrs. Lewison be mistaken about the money? Perhaps Doug got a job and wanted to cut ties with his parents. It was a stretch, but small-town mysteries often were.

Did anyone outside Hotspur, River Run, Dove Crossing, Link, or Junction know of Mariana Nunez's suicide? No. It was a dirty secret, whispered among small-town residents. Lyssa gathered information from Mr. Lewison on how they could stay in contact—just in case Doug ever returned.

21

1991–93

Harry Grist, still employed at the Lewison property, began the arduous process of stripping the tack house of all its reusable equipment and apparatus. Saddles, blankets, harnesses, barrels, troughs—anything horse-related—were sold to local ranchers, farmers, or even art enthusiasts. Large-ticket items went to the Junction, Texas, farm auction. Next came the barn, the tractor, the small backhoe, and the riding lawnmower.

On the day the tack house was demolished, Harry felt a profound sense of unease settle in his gut. Not a man prone to nostalgia, he still quavered deep within. The bulldozer pushed against the building, crushing one side. The structure shuddered and gasped, then collapsed with a cloud of dust as wood splintered and hardware popped. The Lewisons' storeroom met its final demise.

The debris was loaded onto a flatbed and hauled to the far edge of the twenty-acre property, where it was burned in a controlled fire. Afterwards, crews returned with magnetic rakes to collect all the remaining metal fragments. Arthur Lewison had placed Harry in charge and had him hire help for the project.

―――――

"HEY, LOOK HERE," CHARLIE said, pointing to the work board at Atticus' Feed. An ad for part-time help caught his eye. "Maybe I could earn a few extra bucks helping Mr. Grist. What do you think, Dad?"

"Might do, and you can add to your savings for that truck you want. How about we drop by his place on the way home?"

Charlie liked the idea. He and his dad finished loading bags of feed corn and fertilizer for his mom's garden, picked up the vaccines Mr. Koller had ordered, and chatted with a few other customers before heading home—first stop, the Lewison property. Naturally, they made a detour for milkshakes at the new Dairy Queen.

Hotspur had grown. Along with a Sonic and DQ, a new pharmacy—Value Pharmacy—had opened, and a new set of buildings was going up at the edge of town for an animal hospital, catering to horses and guinea pigs alike. Rumors of a new Kroger supermarket excited locals, though Ms. Gilmore and Gilmore Groceries weren't thrilled. She was already planning retirement and the sale of her business.

―――――

CREWS HAD BLOCKED PART of the road leading out to the Lewison property, and Paul Koller swore as he maneuvered around the barricade.

"Charlie boy, remember that summer we went to town and hit the Interstate blacktop after all the county roads?"

"Yes, sir. That fall, Dad—we went to Junction's Lumber store."

"Place sure has changed since then, hasn't it?"

Charlie scanned the area. Cleared land stretched as far as the eye could see. Wood planks, pipes, rebar, concrete, galvanized and PVC cylinders for water drainage, and road crew equipment were stacked in organized piles. Dirt and gravel, surveyors' instruments, and mobile field houses dotted the landscape.

"Yeah, Dad. The place looks like a city now, not a country town. But one thing still looks the same—and still weird to me."

"Oh?" Paul asked as they turned onto the dirt road to the Lewisons' house. "What's that?"

"Those piles of ash-colored brush heaps. I still see a pile of gray bones."

Paul shook his head. Charlie had always had an outstanding imagination. Maybe he should write a scary mystery someday.

———

THE BOYS—NOW NINETEEN AND almost twenty—were ready to face the outside world in many ways, but still not quite prepared. All had stayed close to home, planning or beginning their futures.

Charlie, Bruce, Neal, and Evan donned heavy gloves and began loading crushed, splintered wood onto a flatbed trailer. Harry worked just as hard, sweating and heaving wood alongside the younger guys. Their laughter and camaraderie reminded Harry of Marlin, and the easy bond they had shared. Who knew there'd be this much rubble from a single tack house? The barn remained to be cleared, too.

"You guys remember the tree fort we built in seventh grade?" Charlie asked.

Evan nodded. "Yeah, and man, if we had this much lumber back then, we could've built a fort around the tree and used it as a lookout post."

"Shoot, it would've taken that summer and the next to finish it. You think we'd have still been interested?" Bruce asked.

"Nope," Neal said. "We were interested, just not that kind of interested." He snickered, and the other guys laughed, remembering the mischief of youth. From treehouses to girls, not much had changed in their sense of fun.

———

TWO LARGE HAULS OF cracked concrete revealed dirt beneath the old tack house. Loads of crumbled concrete were separated for disposal. Harry had contacted a company that crushed old concrete to sell to road construction firms—free haul-off, no fuss.

Smaller wood fragments were raked and loaded into a wheelbarrow, then dumped into a converted white Ford pickup, now a mini dump truck. After a dozen loads, Charlie leaned against the truck and took a water break.

He surveyed the area. West of them, old man Glen Adair's place came into view. Charlie remembered him talking for years about getting a wood chipper to mix brush and goat dung into compost. Now, in his late sixties or early seventies, Adair was still spry, methodical, and never in a rush.

"Hey, Bruce," Charlie called.

"Yeah?"

"Let's go ask Glen if he needs help with his brush piles."

"Why, is he planning a controlled burn?"

"Nah, he finally got that wood chipper he's been dreaming about for five years. He's making his own compost."

"Is he hiring?"

"No, Bruce. I just want to do something nice for the old man. He's been a pal to us four guys."

Bruce glanced at Neal and Evan, who were strapping down the lumber. "They're coming out to help too, right?"

"Nope. Neal leaves for vocational school in Austin in two weeks, Evan heads to Fort Worth the following week. They'll be busy preparing to go," Charlie explained.

Bruce shrugged. "Guess I've been outta the loop, huh?"

Charlie sighed. "Growing up also means growing apart."

Bruce, home for a month after two months on an oil rig, muttered, "Some days I wish we were twelve again."

Charlie understood. Life wasn't as simple as it used to be—but he'd keep the Sonic and Dairy Queen.

Those were changes he could handle.

22

THEY WERE DOWN TO the dirt, nails, and wood screws from splintered wood—tiny wood fragments from a felled building.

Grist hopped into the cab that hauled the flatbed, and he and Neal drove off to begin unloading out on the backward ten acres, with Bruce following behind in the converted dump truck.

Evan and Charlie stayed behind, raking and piling up the smaller debris for one last load before they began the burn.

"So, Ev, you and Audra?" Charlie asked as he pulled the rake forward, catching a lot of rubbish and shoving it to one side, then raked from a new direction, repeating the action.

"Yeah. What about us?"

"She going with you? To Fort Worth?"

Evan stopped raking, exhaled, and leaned against the rake handle. "Do you know why I'm headed to Fort Worth? Did I tell you?"

Charlie shook his head. Not looking at Evan, he continued to rake up fragments mixed with dirt and gunk.

"I'm going to enroll in a technical school for communications and stuff, and I'm not moving back."

This statement caused Charlie to stop his raking. "Moving away, Evan? You? Haven't you always said you'd get buried here in Hotspur, because you'd never want to live anywhere else?"

"Come on, Charlie, I said that when I was what, nine? The town is growing, and well, I gotta go where the money is and my dream."

A laugh snorted out of Charlie. "You gotta dream? I never knew that."

"Two of 'em. One is to marry Audra Rafferty, and the other—to be FBI."

Evan Dyer had just unleashed the shock-and-awe feature, leaving Charlie Koller stunned and speechless.

"I got into the video gaming systems, and it's intrigued me, so I've been reading up on software programs and stuff. What surprised me was that it's easy for me, and I have a technical knack."

Charlie shifted to the edge, where bits of broken concrete lay mixed with dirt, the foundation's outline still distinct. He paused and met Evan's gaze. "And, uh, FBI? Where'd that spring from?"

Evan's shoulders lifted, then dropped.

"Watching TV, I guess. I'm not sure. Even so, I'm going to do it—or at least give it my best shot."

"Hey, sounds like a perfect plan, Ev. What does Audra say?"

Evan's face lit up. "That she loves me and, uh, she's moving with me. Only Bruce doesn't know yet, so don't tell him. She's got a job lined up, and we already have a place to live."

Charlie lifted the rake and dug it into the dirt. Loose clods popped up. He repeated the action, embedding the rake head deeper. "So, her parents are okay with this?"

He tugged on the rake, which had gotten stuck on either a buried piece of concrete or a piece of crushed and embedded lumber. Evan moved back and dug his rake in, pulling up more loose dirt mixed with tiny concrete rocks.

"Yeah, they are. Her parents like me. Besides, since my granny died and left me a decent inheritance, they know we won't be living on the streets or eating just ramen noodles."

Evan giggled, stretching his rake out and pulling more debris into the accumulating mound.

"Yeah, it's all you can cook. Hope Audra can cook, or you two will starve." Charlie gave the rake one last heave-ho, dragging up a deteriorating bundle.

"What's that you hooked there, Charlie?"

"Looks like a wad of clothes tied up with a nylon rope."

Evan bent and looked. "Yeah, don't look like nothing good, does it?"

With his work gloves still on, Charlie pinched two fingers together to pick up the bundle and get a better look.

"It's a pair of jeans and, looks like, a faded t-shirt inside, but it feels bulkier than just two articles of clothing."

As the sound of tires rumbling on the side road reached their ears, they looked up just in time to see Grist and Neal arriving on a cleared flatbed truck, followed by Bruce driving an empty dump truck.

Grist was out and headed for the orange Igloo water jug. His old, faded green-and-yellow John Deere cap off his head, he dipped his handkerchief in the metal water tub, wiped his face, then wrapped the dripping cloth around his neck, grabbed a cup, filled it, and chugged.

Neal and Bruce filled their red Solo cups marked with their names, chugged, then refilled.

"Hey'a, what's that there, Charlie?"

Harry replaced the hat on his head and sauntered over to see.

"A bundle of old clothes, we reckon, but we haven't unwrapped it yet. Thinking maybe we should call and get the police out here to check it."

With his pals there, Charlie wasn't as frightened as he would have been if it were just him and Mr. Grist. What was he thinking? Did he think Harry Grist had killed someone and buried the clothes?

Oh my god. What if they dug further down—would they find the body?

As Harry walked closer, Charlie let the bundle hit the dirt and stepped back. Neal and Bruce walked up behind Harry, and Evan stood beside Charlie, clutching the rake handle in a death grip in case he needed a weapon, feeling Charlie's fear radiate outward.

Harry's face squinted in a curious frown. He squatted next to the tied-up bundle, reached into his back pocket, pulled out his work gloves, and slipped them on.

"Neal, get me the long-handled screwdriver outta the cab of the truck, will ya?"

Neal shrugged, retrieved it, and returned.

Harry slipped it under the nylon rope, lifted the pack, and stood. He examined the roll, and, still wearing gloves, pulled at the blue jean material until the rolled-up t-shirt inside was more visible.

Not exposed to sunlight, the shirt was red and a little faded, but still red. He poked the screwdriver into the center of the clothing and pushed out the tip of an old Converse tennis shoe.

On the tip, in dark blue indelible marker, was a large letter **R**. A running joke about Marlin—not knowing his butt end from a hole in the ground, or his left foot from his right. The fellow had been smart-alecky and marked the rips of his shoes with an **L** and an **R**, just to make Harry laugh.

Harry Grist dropped the bundle like it was on fire and fell to his knees, an unearthly cry rising from deep within his chest, thundering out and echoing over the empty acres of land behind them.

The only word the boys understood after that was Harry crying out the name... **Marlin!**

23

MR. LEWISON ALLOWED NEAL Swanson to call the local police department, who in turn contacted the County Sheriff.

"So, what we have are the clothes of this young boy, Marlin Hudson, who you say ran off... what, five years back?" Sheriff Bart McCabe stood erect, arms crossed over his growing middle, his focus fixed on the bundle still lying in the dirt.

Police Chief Toby Grayson looked at Grist and said, "That's the story, Bart. Harry here took the runaway in early spring and wanted to enroll the child in school while he was living with him, but the youngster ran off again. He was hot-footing it to find his dad in San Antonio and wouldn't go to school."

"I recall me and my dad going out to help find him, but he wasn't anywhere to be found that night," Charlie interjected, without being asked.

"You Paul Koller's boy?" Sheriff McCabe eyed him. Small towns—people knew everyone—and he wasn't surprised he recognized Charlie's dad.

"Yes, sir. Charlie... uh, Charles."

"Tell me about that night," Sheriff McCabe said, and they listened as Charlie recounted what he knew. Then they turned their attention to Harry Grist and heard his story. Same story, and McCabe was sure Paul Koller would corroborate it.

McCabe looked over at Mr. Lewison. "Where's your boy Doug? We need to speak to him."

That opened a whole different can of worms.

"So, you're saying your son hasn't had contact with you in at least four years, and you don't know where he is, or this girl, Cathy Nunez, either?"

McCabe scratched the back of his neck, swatting at a buzzing fly, and thought for a moment. "Okay, so we have three persons who vanished out of thin air, and since we have no body—no bones, nothing—we have zero leads."

He looked at the Police Chief. "Toby, get your deputy out here to work the scene. Treat it like a murder investigation. Rope off this area, then we'll bring in some backhoes and dig deeper to see if we can find a body. Bag up that bundle—don't untie it—and get it over to Joyce at my office. I'll have her get the Texas Rangers involved."

McCabe turned to Art Lewison. "Can you get me photos of your son? And who here can get me some information on this girl, Cathy Nunez?"

Charlie lifted his hand.

"Yeah?" the portly sheriff regarded him.

"I know who her best friend was in school; I can ask her for any information she can give you." Charlie knew Lyssa stayed connected with the Nunez family from time to time and hoped this might help find her friend.

The sheriff stood with his hands on his hips, his gun bulkier at his side, right wrist resting atop the pistol belt. He scanned the four boys. Having known their parents for years, he recognized most of the kids.

Harry Grist—yep, he'd known him for over ten years. The Lewisons—new folks; had no dealings with them or their boy. Cathy Nunez—a newcomer, and nobody knew the runaway much at all.

How they all connected was clear to him. They connected on the land owned by Art and Camille Lewison. Were these two at the heart of the mystery? He doubted it, but he'd have Chief Grayson do some digging.

He cleared his throat. "Okay, folks, not much more we can do here. Stop hauling off anything from this site."

"Uh, Chief Grayson," Harry called, getting the man's attention.

"Yeah, Harry, what is it?"

"The barn? Is it okay if me and the boys begin hauling the rubble off?"

Toby Grayson glanced at the smaller barn, now a heap of rubble, then at Sheriff McCabe. "What do you think, Bart? Can they haul it off?"

McCabe swatted at a fly and eyed the distance between the tack shed and barn. "Toby, set the perimeter about ten feet out and tape it off. Anything outside that perimeter, they can haul off or move, including the demolished barn." He looked at Grist. "Harry, if anything else odd pops up, stop and call me."

"Sheriff, are we going to put out a missing person's report?"

"Mr. Lewison, I am. And I'm wondering why you never did that, since you haven't heard from your boy all these years. Later, I'll send one of my officers out to get your full story."

"Well, sir, if you think my wife or I have anything to hide, I assure you we don't. But for reasons of my own, I'll also ask that my attorney be present."

"Fine by me, Mr. Lewison. Reasonable call, since this pile of clothing belonging to a missing runaway was found buried on your property."

The sheriff addressed Grist one last time. "Harry, get me what information you can on that boy. You say he was from Monahans—call their police department, see if his mother filed a runaway report." With that, McCabe got in his car and drove off.

Charlie looked at Evan. "Too bad you aren't already FBI, huh?"

Then Neal looked over. "FBI?"

"Yeah, Ev, what's this about you being FBI?" Bruce asked.

Charlie ducked his head. "Oops, sorry man, didn't mean to let the cat outta the bag."

THE LEWISON HOMESTEAD BECAME a virtual beehive of activity for the next three weeks. Between the Texas Rangers and the sheriff's department, Chief Grayson felt like an overworked yo-yo, with clackers banging against his head.

They hadn't found a body—but it wasn't for lack of digging. Fox holes and ditches were everywhere near the tack house; the place looked like a war zone.

Money was tight for State, County, and City. Lack of funds slowed the search, but flyers went up in all neighboring towns.

Harry had located Mrs. Darnell Harris, formerly Mrs. Jerry Hudson, Marlin's mother, still living in Monahans, Texas, now off drugs and working as a housekeeper in a Motel Six. Her new husband worked as a mechanic for the local trucking company. She'd assumed Marlin was with his dad and had never realized he had disappeared. She provided the most recent photo she had, which was age-enhanced by a forensic artist.

Lyssa reached out to Rey Nunez, who said he'd mail her a picture of Cathy as soon as he dug through old boxes.

"Not sure why you're doing this, Lyssa," Rey said over the phone.

"Because I hope we can find her and make sure she's okay, that's why, Rey."

On the other end, he sighed long and deep.

"Don't you want to find her, Rey?"

"You find her and send her home, and we'll give her a proper burial."

"Oh, my lord, Rey... why do you say that?"

"Because after all these years we haven't heard from her—no letter, no phone call. Lyssa, we know she's dead. My father, brother, sister, and I have already mourned her. You should too. Stop hoping for something that will never come true."

Reynoldo Nunez disconnected, leaving Lyssa speechless, a tear running down her cheek.

———

AFTER FOUR DAYS, EXCAVATION stopped. Harry Grist was tasked with restoring the area: burn off old lumber and haul away debris. Neal and Evan had limited time, so Bruce and Charlie showed up every day to help. Progress was slow without the other two.

"Mr... Harry," Charlie stepped next to him. The older man leaned on his shovel, thoughts elsewhere.

"Oh, sorry. You say something?"

"Could we ask if Lester Hopkins and Preston Boedecker could come out and help? We'd get it done faster with two more sets of hands."

Harry exhaled deeply and rolled his neck. "Nah, Lewison doesn't want more people on his property. He's tired of gossip and stares and doesn't want anyone snooping around. He and his wife hired a company to help sort and pack stuff. In a week, estate planners will sell what they don't care about."

"Oh? When are they leaving?" Charlie asked.

"In another month, maybe two, depending on the sale and legal stuff—especially since they found those clothes."

"Have you heard anything about the forensics or clues from the clothes?"

"Nah, Sheriff McCabe said that takes time, but he's pushing to get it done faster since the Lewisons plan to leave the state."

Charlie frowned. "Does he think they had anything to do with this, is that why he wants to rush it?"

Grist shrugged and shoveled. "Can't say. But he's right—it's their property, and neither can say where their son is, or what they did that night, except that they were sleeping."

"Harry," Charlie's tone was serious. The man stopped and looked at him.

"What's on your mind, boy?"

"That kid, Cathy. Do you think she ran off with Doug? Did you ever see them together?"

Harry's eyes moved across the flat, craggy land in the distance. "Yes, I saw them here together. If I was around, he'd be nice to her—almost a gentleman. Alone, he was mean, a monster."

Charlie's eyes narrowed. "How do you know that if you weren't around?"

"She was bruised a few times, said she fell. I was in the barn loft once when they came in. He smacked her around, had his way with her, even though she said no."

Charlie's anger festered, not just at Doug, but at Harry. "You could've stopped him. Why didn't you?"

"Don't judge me, boy. I was going to. I talked to her, said I'd back up her story and go see Chief Grayson. She said no, begged me to keep quiet. So I did."

Charlie studied his boots, sifting dry dirt, then looked up at the empty land. He exhaled a sad sigh.

"Dirty secrets of a small town, huh?" Grist said.

"No telling, Mr. Grist. But this town isn't as small as it used to be. It's growing. City limits are melting together. Why does it feel like it's closing in on us?"

Charlie had a valid point. Grist didn't answer.

———

DARKNESS FELL. CHARLIE GOT in his dad's old truck, cranked it, and drove onto the white gravel road from the house to the two-lane blacktop. He rolled the window down; it was cooler at night. He watched the flatlands pass in dark blur, headlights the only lights until the first crossroad, now lined with new county streetlamps.

Lights beyond stars and headlights—a weird sensation—made him sad. His simple country life had grown more complicated, crowded, fast-paced, suffocating.

Dragging up that bundle of clothes had changed a lot: town secrets, fear, overpopulation. More bad things could happen because... people were mean. More Doug Lewisons could come. And as growth came, so would danger and fear.

24

"HI, FELLERS, NICE TO see ya," Glen Adair ambled up, wiping the sweat from his forehead with an old red and blue handkerchief that had seen better days.

"Nice to see you, Mr. Adair. Been a while, huh?" Bruce grabbed the old goat's hand and pumped it.

"Lookie at you, Bruce, you sure slimed down, huh. What happened to that chubby little boy I used to know?" Mr. Adair didn't mince words or worry about being politically correct, and Bruce gave the old guy a smile and a half-nod.

"I guess getting taller helped the fat spread out. Still got some love handles, just in case I get me a gal who wants to grab hold."

"Charlie," Adair clapped him on the shoulder, "how's your folks doing?"

"Aw, they're working hard as ever. Mom says she wants some collard greens if you've got any extra, and Libby asked me to tell you to say you don't have any to spare." This made the old guy titter.

"You boys head out back and hop on the tractor; I'm right behind ya. Got the chipper all hooked up and ready to roll."

As they walked ahead, Charlie glanced back at his older neighbor and spotted a slight limp in his gait. He noticed the guy moving a little slower than he had been a week ago. Maybe he and Libby could split checking on the old timer every week. Adair wasn't a spring chicken anymore.

"Charlie, you drive the tractor, will ya? I'll follow you boys in the truck."

———

OUT IN THE BACK twenty, old man Adair had a bulldozer, backhoe, and two hand wagons. He'd been chopping and clearing land where the road ended at the barbed wire fence.

"That road still washing out with the rains?" Charlie stepped up to the fence, his work gloves on, and grabbed it to see how sturdy it was.

"Yep. That last heavy rain nearly washed these brush piles out since they were mostly decomposed. Got a bit of flooding a few weeks back." The old man spat his chew and said, "This road's useless, doesn't go anywhere. Was thinking I might dig myself another stock tank, then graze a few cows back this way."

"You gotta pull this fence down then. You'll need a surveyor to mark off the land, don't this land butt up to the Lewison's?" Charlie rocked the fence post; it was loose from age and weather.

"Yep, sure does, and you're right. But that developer they are selling to has someone marking it off, so I ain't gotta pay for any land survey."

"Works out perfect for you then, no fees." Bruce had his pant legs stuffed into old work boots, took out a pinch of Redman Chew, and tucked it into his cheek. "You guys ready to buzz up some brush?"

THEY'D BEEN AT IT for a few hours, cutting, talking cattle, planting, and of course, goats.

"Gonna see if Atticus Feed will sell some of my homegrown compost for me after I give some to your mom and have her test it out on her garden."

Bruce shoveled another load of wood chips into the flatbed wagon. "Just woodchips and goat dung, that all you're putting in it, Mr. Adair?"

"Why don't you boys call me Glen? I'd like that. And no, I built three compost bins behind my barn. Been using coffee and tree grounds, eggshells, and fruit skins, mixed with grass clippings in one bin. Goat manure and dead leaves mixed with old hay. Chicken droppings and broken eggs from your mom's coops, cow manure from your dad's east pasture that butts up to my land. Got plenty compost now, just hafta add this chipped wood, bag it up, and see what happens."

"Well, dang, Glen, us fellas never knew you were an entrepreneur." Charlie was impressed. So was Bruce.

"I'm not just an old straw-hat-wearing oddball after all," he cackled.

"Alright, dudes, I'm headed over to the trees, gotta take a leak." Charlie followed the barbed wire fence line to a thicker clump of trees for privacy. His back to the others, fly open. He was taking care of business when something silver peeking out from under a clump of dead leaves caught his eye.

Zipping up, he moved away from the wet spot, found a longer limb, and sifted the leaves. It looked like a wad of duct tape. How odd. Something else caught his eye. He yanked gloves from his back pocket, put them on in case a snake lurked under the leaves, and brushed the dried foliage aside. Money—dirty, worn bills. Two fives, a ten, and three ones.

Charlie stood, viewing his find, and looked back at Mr. Adair and Bruce talking and laughing, hard at work. Leave it? Take it? Call the Sheriff? He recovered the bills with the grass and the tape, placed a heavier branch over the pile, found a rock, and marked the spot. His heart pounded. Mr. Adair—no, it couldn't be—he'd known the old man all his life.

———

OLD MAN ADAIR NOTED a subtle change in Charlie's demeanor. "Charlie, you okay?" he asked, taking a rake to the fourth shrinking pile of brush, spreading out a larger limb.

"Oh, sure, just getting hungry," Charlie lied, mind on the tape and money. How had it gotten out here? Carried by someone, but who?

"Let's stop, grab a bite, take a quick break," Adair said, wiping sweat from his brow.

They went back to Adair's house, made sandwiches, drank sweet tea, and chatted about nothing. Mr. Adair shared stories from his life and the war, the boys listening attentively.

"Okay, fellas, let's get another few hours of wood chipping then call it a day, you game?" Adair stood and plunked his wide-brimmed straw hat on, his wrinkled face smiling.

The boys nodded, grabbing their hats, gloves, and shades, and followed him out to the back twenty to finish the old piles of brush.

"MY LORD, NEVER THOUGHT we'd get to the start of this darned pile, but we're almost there," Bruce said, marking his spot with a shovel.

Charlie found the dirt rake, put his gloves back on. "Only six more piles to go. How about we finish this one and quit until later?"

They'd cleared four rather large piles since Adair seemed to want skyscraper-sized brush piles, not just tall, but wide.

Adair spat a wad of tobacco juice, leaving a darker stain on his lips. "Seems I got heavy-handed on a few of these piles. Sorry, fellers. Let's do one more. Looks like rain's coming; we won't work for a day or two until the brush dries out."

Charlie and Bruce both glanced at the gray sky toward the north. Adair was right—rain was coming. Charlie's next thought: the tape and dirty old money. He needed to bag it.

"Then let's get this done before the rains arrive." Charlie raked small debris, piling it for Bruce to shovel into the wheelbarrow, while Adair cleared the chipper and started the next pile.

A steady, silent rhythm developed. None of the three added much idle talk; even Bruce, usually the clown, was quieter than normal. Charlie felt a heaviness in his chest, something he'd only felt twice before—once when Frannie Swisher went missing six or seven years ago, and again a few days back when that bundle of clothes was unearthed.

Thumps and hammering echoed as the chipper de-voured limbs and brush, pulverizing smaller pieces into sand. Glen's large square-point shovel lifted mounds into his truck, Bruce wheeled the last bit of debris filled with dirt, tamping it down with the back of his shovel.

The pile was shrinking when a rat snake slithered out, startling Bruce and Charlie. Both jumped back, shovels and rake at the ready, hearts racing.

Bruce cursed. "Shoot, scared the dickens outta me! I hate snakes."

"Me too. Glad it wasn't a rattler," Charlie said, reach-ing with his rake to pull in a pile of brush. His rake caught a foreign object, which flew at him, hit his chest, then dropped at his feet. He looked down—a human skull. His heart stopped, legs felt like bags of rocks, eyes glued to the skull. He swallowed, then found his voice.

"Stop! Stop digging, Bruce! Now! Glen! Glen! Mr. Adair!" His words carried over the chipper's noise. "Turn off the chipper!"

Glen heard him the second time, worry creasing his forehead. Had one of the boys been hurt? He rushed over.

Adair felt sick. It was his property. Would they think he had anything to do with this? Before they got into the truck, Charlie told him about the tape and money. He retrieved it, wrapping it in an old unused kerchief from Glen's truck.

From Adair's kitchen, Charlie dialed the police sta-tion, Bruce and the old man standing next to him. All three were shaken at the discovery of human remains on Adair's land.

"Hotspur police station, may I help you?"

"Hey, Tiff, it's Charlie. Is the chief in?"

"Hey, yeah. Let me get him."

"Charlie. What can I do for you?" Toby Grayson said, leaning back in his chair, propping a foot on the desk, then sitting up straight as Charlie explained what he'd uncovered on Adair's land.

25

"Two skeletons?" Toby Grayson took a step back as his two deputies and staff from the local funeral home worked at excavating the area. It wasn't just the amount they'd found—since the human body has 206 bones—it was the second skull that sealed the deal.

When Glen Adair heard that, he all but passed out, and Charlie's hand moved out to steady the old fella.

"Two? Oh, lord, oh lord, how... and on my land, Chief? How could this have happened?" Glen was beside himself. "Are you gonna arrest me?" His usually deep-tanned and wrinkled face paled; he aged twenty years in a matter of seconds.

Toby Grayson had known Glen Adair since he was in short pants. The man had lived in River Run before moving to Hotspur. He and his late father Butch were members of a small Farming Association back in the early seventies. No way would he ever believe this old dude was a killer—but the people who were his land neighbors, the Lewisons... how about them? Or even Harry Grist?

"No, Glen, I'm not arresting you. We will have to go over some questions later. You can relax."

The aged guy let out a pent-up breath, and his entire old body sagged; thankfully, Charlie had a hold of him.

"Uh, Chief," the deputy got his attention. "We've got a shoe and some degraded clothing here... looks like a shirt and shorts."

"Bag them and be careful," the police chief said, frowning and thinking about the one shoe. One shoe. Hadn't that Swisher girl's one shoe been all they'd found back in 1986? What were the odds? He let loose a thoughtful sigh and knew as soon as he got back to the station, he would call Sheriff McCabe.

Charlie helped Adair get situated inside the front seat of his truck, leaving the door open so the old guy could get air.

"Bruce, stay with Glen. I want to talk to Toby."

"Yeah, sure, back here is fine with me." Bruce, shaken up at this gruesome find, wanted some distance.

Charlie stepped up next to Grayson.

"Uh, Chief, can I have a word?"

"Sure." The chief's eyes stayed on the digging and bagging.

"Back here." Charlie stepped away from other ears.

Grayson's brow puckered, but he took the few steps backward.

"What's up?"

Charlie described the tape and the money, watching the questions ripple across the chief's face.

"Where did you say you found it? Show me." Before he left, he waved at Deputy Yarrow.

"Hey, Chad, be back in a minute."

Chad Yarrow looked back and gave an affirmative head nod. "Sure, Chief."

Toby and Charlie walked to the barbed-wire fence that stopped at the county road.

"Under this pile of leaves, just on the other side of the fence." Charlie pointed.

"You got gloves with you?"

"Yeah, here." Charlie handed him work gloves, and Toby used them to hold the barbed wire together to get over the fence, then handed them back to Charlie.

"You search the area thoroughly?"

"No, sir."

Toby looked around, found a longer skinny limb, and poked about. He carefully moved dead leaves and twigs and zeroed in on something. In a squat, he put on a latex glove and shifted some debris over, spotting the broken zip tie, then another. He stood.

"Welp, Charlie, I think you stumbled on a crime scene."

If Charlie Koller had had a potty mouth, several unacceptable words would have flown. All he could say was, "You're kidding me?"

"Nope. You mind going back and getting Chad, uh, Deputy Yarrow," Grayson adjusted, to be more official. "Ask him to bring crime scene tape, okay?"

"Yes, sir."

"Oh, Charlie, be discrete. Let's not alarm anyone else, not until I get the Sheriff notified."

Charlie nodded and turned to leave, his heart stuck in his throat. Crime scene: this was unreal.

The next few days, Adair's land swarmed with the Sheriff's department personnel, a few people from the State Police, and members of the county medical examiner's office.

All the bones found had been taken to the Department of Public Safety's forensic laboratory in Austin, Texas.

A woman highly sought after for her expertise in facial reconstruction, who worked for the Department of Public Safety, received these two skulls and began her work.

Hotspur's Chief of Police already had photos of Frannie Swisher and Cathy Nunez, since they'd both been reported missing.

Harry Grist was questioned, and he was able to describe Marlin Hudson to the forensic artist. Afterward, Chief Grayson called Marlin's family in Monahans, Texas, and was able to locate the father in San Antonio.

Abe Hudson was incarcerated in Three Rivers Prison. He'd been there for three years, serving a twenty-year sentence for first-degree robbery. The kid would have never found him had he gotten to San Antonio.

Unsure of Doug's whereabouts since the Nunez girl's disappearance, Camille and Art Lewison shared a photo of him, assuming he'd also vanished. Their son hadn't contacted them about needing more money. This, they explained to the police chief, clarified why they hadn't filed a missing person's report.

Toby thought it odd, but they explained their son was of age. What were they supposed to do?

Camille went pale when the chief stated the girl wasn't of age.

"Didn't you think about that at all?" the chief asked, tone accusatory.

"Well, no sir, we didn't. Did the mother ever file a report?"

Toby Grayson's face hardened. "No," he answered curtly.

He knew the poor Nunez woman was distraught. She had told him she knew where her daughter was and couldn't force her to return home. Mrs. Nunez said her daughter would just keep running away, putting her through this misery repeatedly.

It was two weeks later that Maria Nunez hung herself.

"If by any chance your son reaches out, call me."

Grayson handed his card to Art, staring hard at the man. Mr. Lewison was a cold fish.

He left them, passing Harry Grist, who also sent off vibes the chief could not ignore.

In his car, he cranked the engine and sat, letting it idle in the circular driveway. Large home, well decorated; yet not as cared for as he figured.

He knew the property was for sale and they were moving—but why tear down the barn and the tack house?

If they had been part of the boy's demise, or knew about it, they would have never bulldozed the tack house, keeping that clump of clothing hidden.

Now, he thought, the chances of finding the skeletons—the odds were ten to one, decent odds. Adair was a 'neat' landowner and a rarity, conscientious of the ecosystem.

Adair hated an unsightly mess even if it were dead brush or fallen trees. Fallen trees became firewood, dead brush he burned off, or in this case he chipped and mixed with goat droppings for a natural fertilizer and manure-free mulch.

The tape and the money that Charlie discovered were more worrisome.

Degraded as they were, they had still found two viable hairs stuck to the inside folded sticky part. This would be stored and protected for further DNA testing if possible.

The money, though... shoot... he knew people in these parts were careful about money, careful because they had very little of it.

The Lewisons had money, though, and more than normal. Did they have disregard for it?

He was sure the boy, who he'd heard stories about, did. No one in the high school liked him; this he'd heard from his sixth-grade daughter, Lulu. According to Lulu, he was cute but a snotty brat, a showoff with money.

Just about to press the accelerator after engaging the car into drive, he glanced up at the house and saw a curtain move. The fingers were of a man—Art Lewison.

Why was he watching him?

Toby felt that something was off.

The issues Chief Grayson and law enforcement faced were: They had four people unaccounted for, and only two skeletons... were there more to be found? If so, where did they start? It was not practical to dig up the entire acreage of one old man named Glen Adair, so what was the next step?

An idea formed three days later.

In the small red-brick police building, Toby shut the door to his office and pulled over his Rolodex.

"Hey, Paula, it's Toby. Is Sal in?"

"Yep, hold on, Chief."

"Toby! Good to hear from you. What's up?"

"Sal, you heard about this stuff going on, and I need a favor, if you can."

Sal listened as the Chief of Police explained.

"So, you want me to contact Nate Swanson, Paul Koller, Len Dyer, and old man Adair and have them file injunctions? All against the Lewisons' property sale?"

"Yep, until I get this sorted out. I'd prefer these folks to remain in Texas, and I'm hoping this gets them to stay so they can fight this in court."

"Geezers, Toby, on what grounds?"

"Sal, just trust me for once, will ya?"

"Just because you're the chief of police, baby brother, don't mean you can boss me." Sal grinned into the phone.

One kid became a cop, the other a lawyer who managed a lucrative business handling the legalities of market farmers, dairy farmers, ranchers, and store owners in the area of Hotspur, River Run, and Dove Crossing, including the Auction House in Link. Occasionally, he handled private matters as well—last wills and testaments and such.

"Sure, if you have that gut feeling, lil bro. Let me reach out, see what I can do. I have a few buddies who are surveyors in that neck of the woods. Maybe these douchebag developers can focus on building the roads up before they bring in the gaggle of folks they think are going to flock to this area."

"Thanks, Sal, I owe you one. How about you, Gina, and the kids come over next Saturday? Steaks on the grill, cola for the kids, and beer for us?"

"You're on, as long as we get some homemade ice cream, and I'll get Tilly to make her famous potato salad and baked beans."

"Deal. And Sal, really, thanks," said Toby before hanging up.

26

THE FORENSIC TEAM IN San Antonio worked overtime.

This small-town issue had become big news, and people had eyes on Hotspur's Chief of Police, the Sheriff, and the State Police.

What the forensics lab found stunned everyone, as well as perplexed them.

The bones were of a teenage boy and girl.

Marlin Hudson was the only boy they had heard about. But why him?

The girl, however, could either be the Nunez girl or the Swisher girl; and the tennis shoe matched the shoe found in Link, Texas, near the Auction House.

During the first search, several teeth were found, and Grayson had asked that a second team be sent out to further search for small teeth and bones.

They were having a lucky streak; several teeth were recovered in the mess of debris.

These were then matched to dental records, thus proving Frannie Swisher was the female skeleton.

The facial reconstruction confirmed her identity.

Once they'd finished with all the testing, documenting, and photographing, her bones were sent home to Iron River, Wisconsin, so her family could lay her to rest.

How awful for Jessica Mae Swisher, who was now five years old, born six weeks after Frannie's abduction. Poor Jessie was meeting her big sister for the first and last time of her life.

Sadness shadowed that small town as it filled with family members and friends to say one last goodbye.

After a photograph and dental records of Marlin Hudson confirmed the young male skeleton was him, his mother, stepfather, and siblings came to carry him back to Monahans.

Attorney Sal Grayson spent this time drafting legal letters to stop two things: the Lewisons from closing on the sale of their property, and the developers from swooping in and changing any landscape to cover up whatever else might be hidden on this land.

"CAN THEY DO THAT?" Camille's face twisted in anger.

Art's fingers went from left to right on the letter as he re-read it again.

"Looks like it, Honey, and it seems legal, too."

Harry Grist stood inside the doorway, on one of the rare occasions he'd been in the house, still not asked to sit or make himself at home.

"Seems our neighbors have some land issues they are taking up with us—property zoning, easements, and underground watering issues—and have halted the sale until further surveying can be done."

Camille huffed.

"At their expense, not ours. Maybe that'll have them change their minds. This is pure bullshit."

Harry Grist's brows raised at her language, but he agreed with her. Why were they doing this?

He knew these people; they weren't like this, never had been.

He was going to keep mum about it, but he figured it was the police chief and his doing. Toby was smart, and he had something up his sleeve.

"Well, I am not going to just sit here and do nothing. I'll call our attorney in Los Altos Hills, see what he has to say."

Camille made to rise, but Art placed his hand on her arm, and she stayed seated.

"Don't bother, Dear."

"And just why not?" She frowned at her husband.

"Texas laws versus California laws. I'm sure there are differences, and we'll have to abide by this state's laws. Let's just ride it out; it can't take forever."

Harry was still standing there. He cleared his throat to get their attention.

"Sir, will you still want me staying on?"

Before Camille could speak, Art stood and faced their hired hand.

"Yes, Mr. Grist, if you will. We still have to oversee the rest of the cleanup, and I'd like some help with moving things around in the wine cellar. You can also help with packing our personal things and houseware. Plus, there are odd chores you can do until this mess is cleared up."

A whine emitted from Camille.

"I'll take care of the packing."

"No, you've been slowing down, I've noticed, and you are out of breath a lot. No need to overdo it. Besides, I'm sure Mr. Grist appreciates being paid wages until we are out of the state."

"Yes, sir, that I am. Thank you. I'll go tend to the rented equipment, move it around so we can restart tomorrow."

Grist plopped that old green John Deere cap on his head, turned, and walked to the back toward the mudroom.

Just as he grabbed the doorknob, he heard Arthur Lewison call out, "Oh, Mr. Grist, wait a minute, please."

"Harry," Art hailed him by first name.

"You know what has to be done. Can you do it?"

"There are lots of eyes on this right now, but I'll do what I can. Not positive I can do both, though."

His frown was that of concern, not anger.

"How far out is the girl?"

Art looked over Grist's shoulder out the half-glass on the back door.

"Near the fence line. Too far to drive a backhoe or dozer and not raise suspicions, but it'll be years before the developers get back that way to clear off land and begin excavating, I'm sure of that. What does Mrs. Lewison think?" were Harry's next words.

Mr. Lewison's eyes widened.

"Are you joking? I haven't told her. The woman would have a stroke. My wife can never know, nor shall she."

Harry's hand came up and he rubbed his forehead, then raked his hand down his face, pulling his old skin.

"You got me implicated in this mess. Don'tcha think I deserve an explanation, sir?"

"Not now. Mrs. Lewison is waiting in the other room, but yes, you do. Let's get this business in the cellar taken care of first. I need you to figure out what we can do. I mean, where we can dispose of, uh, it."

"Mr. Lewison, why now? Why do we gotta move it? We weren't planning to before, were we?"

"Because, Mr. Grist, this legal action changes things. I know it was the Chief of Police, that Toby Grayson, who called in this injunction on the selling of our property, and if he gets his way, they might just strip this house down to the ground."

Harry Grist shrugged.

"If you say so, guess you know best."

Art nodded, turned, and left Grist to see himself out the door.

Camille was still at the dining room table, hands in her lap, face forward, her eyes glued on the hand-painted print hanging on the wall.

Art watched her, her eyes unblinking, her lips in a flat straight line, her cheekbones sunken, her color pallor.

He pulled out the chair and sat next to her, resting his elbows on the tabletop.

She inhaled.

"Art, you know, I know, don't you?"

"About what, Dear?"

"What about him, my Dear?" His pulse quickened.

"He is responsible for those skeletons. It was him, just like California."

Her hands twitched in her lap as she wrung them in anguish, her voice trembling.

"Yes, Sweetheart, it was him; like before."

"Art, I'm sure he's heard about this news. What if he does come back? Are you still afraid of him?"

Camille gave her husband an unhappy glance, watching his reactions to her question, with unasked questions of her own.

Art refused to meet his wife's eyes, but he moved his hand to hold hers.

"No, Dear, I'm not."

27

THE CELLAR MOVE WAS not what Grist expected.

"In the daylight? Are you crazy?"

"Look, Grist. Camille's going to be in Junction for half a day this morning, and we need to move the wine racks before she discovers your dig site. My wife likes her wine, and if I tell her she can't come down here, she'll get suspicious. It was hard enough when I told her she couldn't when we buried him the first time. Got any ideas on how we can hide the fact that we moved the racks over?"

Art Lewison wrung his hands in worry.

Harry Grist swallowed and exhaled.

"We can say one cracked and we had to repair it. Where do you want me to rebury it?"

It. Grist called Doug. It. Not that he figured Art cared, but saying the words—'rebury your son'—felt wrong.

"Back near the girl. Like you'd said before, near the boundary of my land and the state's property. You're right, Harry. I checked on zoning, and it's zoned for state use only. Future roads and such will be constructed, and by then, those involved would be dead, including me."

Grist said nothing. He was now part of this mess, and had been since the girl. So what was he going to do? He could not call the police chief and explain.

"I thought about taking him with us back to California, but then I'd have to tell Camille, and I just can't—not yet."

Harry Grist saw the defeat in Lewison's eyes.

"They are digging into those skeletons and that bundle of clothing, so what if they come out here to nose around?" Harry asked his employer.

"The Police, or the sheriff? They have no just cause and I don't care. My wife is ill, and I'm ready to just walk away from this all and let it sit and rot. Leave him where he is and send an anonymous letter with a map to her body, too."

"You do that, and it implicates me. I'm already gonna be outta work when you leave, so..." Harry left that hanging in the air, staring at the man.

Lewison exhaled and gritted his teeth a fraction.

"You'll be rightly compensated for your help and your silence, not to worry."

He left Grist to tend to his wife. The lawyers were still in a battle, the surveyors weren't done, and he was sick of everyone dragging their feet; the police chief's relentless watchful eyes had burned a hole through him.

———

His phone rang.

"Chief, there's a Mrs. Van de Bern on line three. Says she's from Los Alto Hills, California, wants to talk with you."

"Put her through."

"Mrs. Van de Bern, Chief Grayson, how may I help you?"

Her story... wow... Had Doug Lewison been involved
and gotten away with murder in California, in 1983?
They had no real proof, but the conjecture... it was
compelling.

Mrs. Martin Van de Bern was a wealth of information; it spilled out of her mouth, and Chief Grayson
scribbled as fast as he could, hoping he could read his
scrawl later.

"Yarrow, you and Tiff come in here." Grayson sat
back, reading the names on the list. Would they still be
in the California area, with the same phone numbers?

"Yeah, chief?" Both his office receptionist and deputy
stood at his doorway.

"Chad, take this list and see how many of these numbers are still good. We're two hours ahead of them, so
if you get someone on the phone and I'm here, I want
to talk to them. If I'm not here, ask them when I can
call them back. Got it?"

"Yes, sir," said Chad, taking the list from him to go
get started.

"What do you want me to do, Chief?"

"Call the Los Altos Police Department. Ask for the
homicide division and see if you can get us a copy of
the murder book and any reports on a Missy Van de
Bern, back from the fall of 1983."

"They might ask me why I want it, Toby."

"Tell them I spoke with a Mrs. Martin Van de Bern,
and she told me to reach out to Detective Gonzales.
He's the one who worked her daughter's case. If you
can get him on the phone, then I'd like to talk to him."

"This got anything to do with these bones, Chief?"

"I do not believe so, but there is a connection
through the missing boy, Doug Lewison."

"I'm on it," Tiff said and turned to leave, but stopped when Toby called her back.

"Tiff."

"Yes, sir?"

"You still in contact with any of the girls from the high school?"

Tiffany Henderson had been involved with the cheer squad and the twirlers a few years back when she taught dance.

"Some of them that are still here that didn't go off to college. Why?"

"Any of them have any dealing with this Doug person, or maybe Cathy Nunez, the missing girl?"

"Yeah, Toby, one I know did. Lyssa Caldwell."

"She still lives here in Hotspur?"

"Yeah, she dates Charlie Koller." Tiff smiled. "They are the cutest couple."

"Call her. I want to talk to her, will ya?"

"Sure thing, Toby."

Chief Grayson sat back.

This kid, Doug... If he was the culprit, where was he?

A person like this, suspected of committing a crime from 1983, has a history.

He needed to work backwards and find out about this boy.

Two sets of remains, one girl who'd vanished, and a girl named Missy Van de Bern. The Van de Bern girl's homicide was a crime still unsolved.

Was the kid connected?

If so, then this boy had a history of other things.

Hotspur Chief of Police, Toby Grayson, was positive.

THE DAY AFTER REACHING out to the Los Altos Homicide Department, Detective Manny Gonzales called.

"Chief, a Sergeant Detective Gonzales from Los Altos is on line two." Tiff called out through the open door.

"Got it, Tiff, thanks." Toby lifted the receiver and pushed line two.

"Chief Grayson."

"Chief Grayson, this is Sergeant Detective Manny Gonzales from the Los Altos homicide division. I got a note here that you wanted to discuss the Missy Van de Bern case from 1983. That correct?"

"Yes, Sergeant Detective Gonzales, it is, and please, call me Toby."

"Okay, Toby, and I'm Manny. What do you want to know?"

Grayson went into his questions and then listened as Manny expounded a little.

"The reason Doug Lewison was on our radar is that he'd been stalking the poor girl after she declined an invitation to a school dance. Other students saw it, too—they said he had a huge crush on her and followed her around, at school and after school.

"Mrs. Van de Bern lodged a complaint because they were getting phone calls from him. He wanted to talk to Missy, and her parents told us she was too scared to answer.

"The few times she did talk to him, he was polite at first. But after she told him she wasn't interested—didn't want a boyfriend—he got nasty. Belligerent.

"At school, he acted sweet until she rejected him in public. Loudly, as we were told. That's when he started acting out, menacingly.

"I have to stress, though—this is all conjecture. No proof. No witnesses came forward."

Toby pressed the phone to his ear.

"Menacing in what ways? Can you elaborate?"

"Yes. It started, the Van der Berns said, with phone calls late at night. No one was there, just heavy breathing, then hanging up. One night Missy found a dead cat on the rear porch, and two nights later a kitten. The kitten was strangled with a red ribbon, and the cat was stabbed in the heart with a large concrete nail."

"And how did this relate to Doug Lewison?" Toby was a little confused, and he heard Manny Gonzales sigh over the phone.

"Because several years ago neighbors of the Lewisons all filed reports of pets disappearing; and a few animal carcasses were found later in an area also close to their home. Several neighbors pointed a finger at the Lewison kid, but again, there was no positive proof. His parents vouched for him and said their son would never harm an animal, but ..."

"But? But what, Manny?"

"We interviewed him, Toby, and I saw something in his eyes, or rather I didn't see something."

"What was that?"

"No conscience, or remorse at the mention of dead animals, like puppies or kittens, and I swear, the child seemed, well, soulless."

Toby cringed at that, then asked Manny,

"What are his parents like?"

"I don't know. Well, wait, let me explain that better. These people, Camille and Arthur Lewison, aren't his biological parents; they are related because they are his aunt and uncle."

"Where's his mom and dad, then?"

"Both are dead. The mother, Lucinda Drake, killed her husband, Gordon, and then herself when the child was almost one. The mother's medical records stated she was a manic-depressive with schizophrenia. Her paranoia caused her to be institutionalized until she was seventeen. Then we learned that the father, Gordon, was bipolar and on medication. Listen, Toby, this is information not to be shared with the boy."

"I can manage that, Manny, because he's missing, has been for a few years now."

"What? Missing, how?"

Chief Grayson explained the situation, and about the girl, Cathy Nunez. He then explained the skeletal remains found and the heap of clothing.

"What a tangled mess you've got for yourself there, Chief."

"Yeah, same thing I was thinking, Manny. Listen, back then, did the boy have any friends, a best friend, anything you know of?"

"Only one, but that boy moved off just before Missy Van de Bern was killed. His name was Ryan Chapin. They moved to Santa Cruz County."

"Manny, do you have any idea on how to reach this Chapin boy?"

"Yep, as a matter of fact, I have his parents' contact and his, too. He was going to city college, and I'm not sure he is still living at home, though."

"This is perfect. It gives me a start. Now, back to this Missy, what happened that you suspected Doug Lewison?"

"After the dead kitten incident, it stopped for right at two weeks, and we were told that Doug ignored Missy and her friends, and became isolated at school. Headed into the third week, the heart of a dead dog was put in Missy's best friend's locker along with a note that said, 'This heart belongs to my best friend, and soon, the heart of your best friend will be missing, forever gone from you.'

That Saturday, after a class party, Missy vanished. Search teams hunted for her for three weeks, and there wasn't a ransom call, so everyone felt the worst had happened. That boy, Lewison, joined a search team and acted all morose and worried, and he was even trying to comfort her mother."

"Was it five weeks later you found her body?"

"At the docks, under some old wooden lifeboats by a fish hatchery. The dead fish guts, and stuff masked the smell of a decomposing body. A few of the employees had brought their sons to work one Saturday, and the boys were playing pirates and asked if they could turn one of the lifeboats over to use. They picked just the right one to uncover her body. It was bad, Toby, terrible. Her initial cause of death the medical examiner said was strangulation with a garrote, and it broke her hyoid bone."

"Strangulation is a vicious way to kill another person. It's up close and personal and reflects a certain dominance over the victim; and the killer can watch the life of their victim ebbing away."

"Yeah, it's a psychological form of domination, I agree. I've worked on a couple of strangulation cases. Domestic violence where it was charged with passion and based on a husband and wife, or boyfriend, girlfriend scenario, but this girl, Missy, no, the person who did this was a sadistic killer. After she was dead, he took a scaling knife and carved out her heart and lay it on her chest and that had us back looking at the letter."

"Did you lift prints off the letter, and what made you think it was Lewison?"

"He was the first person we suspected because of the stalking, the phone calls, and the dead critters found. The note was printed on a school test paper written by Martin Schulder. It had been the teacher's file. Papers she graded to hand back to the students. Her prints were on it, so were Martin's, so were Doug's and one other student's, a Bernice Phelps."

"Wasn't that proof enough?" Toby was confused.

"No, because those test papers were touched by over four people. Martin sat behind Doug. The teacher asks everyone to pass their test forward, to get them to the first person in the row. Martin passed his to Doug who handed the entire seven student row's papers to the teacher. The teacher, Miss Freeman, says she keeps all papers in grading folders on top her desk, all students there had access to that folder. So, we could not point a straightforward finger at the kid."

"But he was the one who was terrorizing her."

"Yes, and Missy Van der Bern was no angel herself. She was a bit of a snooty rich kid, too. There were a handful of kids that she tormented, and guess what, Martin Schulder was one of them, along with Bernice Phelps, who Miss Freeman asked to help her organize all test papers from three different classes that day."

"I see. And the crime scene. No prints?"

"No. It rained at the docks several days in a row, and that particular area flooded, so any prints got washed away."

"Did the medical examiner get anything usable, anything at all, back then?" Toby had his fingers crossed.

"Under the fingernail scrapings, but not much more than that; and without a comparison to match to, won't help us much."

"Well, Manny, this has been insightful, and there is one thing I am sure of."

"Oh, what's that, Toby?"

"It would suit me if Doug Lewison continued to be missing. He sounds like a monster."

Sergeant Detective Manny Gonzales breathed into the mouthpiece of the phone and said,

"I am with you there, Chief Grayson, one hundred percent."

28

"WHY WOULD CHIEF GRAYSON want to talk to me? I know nothing about what happened." Lyssa's voice filled with stressful worry.

Charlie scooched closer, took her hand, lacing their fingers, and squeezed. "I wouldn't worry, babe. I'm sure it's nothing. When Tiff called, did she mention why?"

Lyssa Caldwell expelled a long breath; her body sagged and then rested against Charlie's.

"It's because I was friends with Cathy Nunez, and she says the Chief wants to talk to people who were close to her. Charlie, I do not want to disclose any of her personal secrets. I don't want people to think horrid things about Cathy even if she's dead." A tear dropped from one eye, then the other.

"Look, Lyssa. Tell them what you know. Don't worry. It's not like you are hurting her, but just getting her story out there."

"Charlie?"

"Yeah?"

"I hope this doesn't scare you."

This comment had him turning his head to look at her. "Lyssa, are you okay?"

"Yes, more than okay. I love you, you know?"

"That works out perfect," he said, his voice a soft murmur as a smile filled his senses. His face shining with emotion, he added, "because I love you, too."

It wasn't their first kiss by far, but it was the first one after their declaration of love, and it felt like a first kiss—the passion more intense, yet sweet. The kiss ended, but Charlie's arm stayed around her shoulder, and he hugged her close.

"Listen, I'll go with you when you go talk to the Chief."

"I told Tiff I'd come by this afternoon after work. I'll be fine." Lyssa looked at her watch. "Lord, I need to go, or I'll be late for work, sorry."

Charlie stood, taking her by the hand. "I'll walk you to your car."

He kissed her goodbye through the open window. "Drive safe and call me tonight."

A look passed between them, negating the need to repeat the words 'I love you.' Sometimes unspoken declarations of love were that much stronger.

Paul Koller's truck passed Lyssa's car, and they both waved. He was carrying a package of vaccines for the new calves—ones they hadn't expected this June.

When he found out three of his heifers were pregnant, Paul's response had been humorous: "Well, when the urge hits, you've got to scratch that itch, even if you're a heifer who falls in love with our one stud of a bull, like your mom did with me."

"Paul Koller, you stinker," Lindy remarked, giving him a punch and blushing, causing Charlie and Libby to make the oh-my-god faces.

"I like that lil gal, Charlie boy." He cradled the box of vaccines and the syringes, along with four bottles of water and a lunch sack with two ham sandwiches and two bags of chips—a tradition for father and son to eat lunch under the large oak tree in the south pasture where the new momma heifers were grazing.

"Hey, Dad, when's Gregg coming home for a visit? I heard Mom say he called."

"Next month. He's taking a three-week leave and spending two weeks here."

"What about the other week? Did he tell Mom his plans?"

Paul beamed. "Your big brother is going to Galveston with his new girlfriend."

"Gregg has a new girlfriend? Really? Man, I thought he'd be pining away for that girl over in Dove Crossing for eternity. You know, what's her name, uh, Janna Mattison?"

"Nope. Libby told your mom that Janna got married and is living in San Antonio now. She said Gregg's heart was crushed."

Charlie's face creased in a frown. "How does Libby know all this?"

A laugh spewed out of his father's mouth. "Your sister seems to have her finger on the pulse of the Link Connection."

"What the heck is a Link Connection?" Charlie asked in confusion.

"Our town, River Run, and Dove Crossing are connected at points by Link, and that's what Libby calls it—the Link Connection. Anyway, she keeps her ears open wide these days."

Further baffled, Charlie asked, "Why does she keep her ear to the ground? Is she turning into an old biddy gossip?"

"Since Frannie Swisher vanished, then Cathy Nunez, she's gotten paranoid. Then this stuff about the bones and, with that rich kid who disappeared, your sister's been worried. According to her, a lot of crazy things happen in rural towns, but they only become public knowledge when a film is made about them. By staying informed about everyone and everything, she says that ensures all our safety and security."

"My sister is a lunatic and a worrywart." Charlie huffed. "Does she know who Gregg's new girl is?"

"Of course, and you know her too—Tara Swanson."

"No kidding? Wow, she's a pip of a girl," Charlie giggled. "Gregg will have his hands full with her."

Charlie and Tara's brother, Neal, had been best friends since fourth grade. He once had a crush on Tara, although she was almost three years his senior. She was a real farm girl—rode better than a boy, could even calf rope, and wasn't afraid of hard work or dirt. She was also sexy. A pair of boot-cut jeans and a button-down shirt tied at the waist looked amazing on her.

His thoughts turned to Lyssa Caldwell, who had a figure that rocked the same look. His gal Lyssa and Tara were a lot alike—both country girls with the land in their souls and ranching and farming in their veins.

Wow. Brothers with girlfriends way out of their league ... talk about an amazing stroke of luck!

"Hiya, Tiff." Lyssa let the door shut behind her. Her palms were sweaty, and she swallowed hard. "Chief Grayson ready to see me?"

Tiffany looked up and saw a nervous and pale Lyssa Caldwell. "Gosh, girl, don't be scared. You aren't in trouble."

"Oh, I know. It's just, well, I've never been interviewed by a police chief or anything, you know?"

Toby Grayson's voice carried into the outer room. "Tiff, send Ms. Caldwell in. I'm ready for her."

"Charlie! Lyssa's on the telephone!" Libby shrieked from the kitchen.

He picked up the extension in the family room, waiting for the click from his sister hanging up. No click.

"Libby," he said, "this is not a three-way call. Hang up, please."

"Oh. Alright, I will. But before I do, Lyssa, you off work tomorrow?"

"Yeah, why?"

"How about riding fences with me tomorrow? I'd like the company." Libby asked with her fingers crossed.

"Sure. Can you wait until about eight? I'm getting up early to help Mom with making bread and butter pickles with her first batch of cucumbers before she heads off to work."

On the other end, Charlie tossed in, "Tell her I want a jar. Now, Libby, hang up the phone."

"Bye, Lyssa. See you tomorrow." Libby clicked off, and Charlie waited a two-second beat before saying, "Hi beautiful, how was your afternoon?"

She explained how the interview with the Chief of Police went and felt more at peace. Even though some of the things she disclosed about Cathy's physical relationship with Doug Lewison were a tad embarrassing, she did it.

"I'm proud of you, Honey," Charlie said. "Even though we don't know if Doug is still alive," he paused, "and for that matter Cathy, either. You know, no physical bodies or, uh, bones have been found like the ones on Mr. Adair's land."

"After my talk with the chief I'd say the odds aren't in favor of a positive outcome with them both missing all this time. But..." she paused. "Well, I asked Chief Grayson something and it's odd how he answered."

"What'd ya ask him?"

"Well, if it was Doug that was responsible for the two skeletons—that boy, Marlin, and Frannie Swisher—why wasn't Cathy there too, if it was him that killed her? And if it was, and now he's gone without a trace, then I figure he's left the country, and that's why he can't be found."

"You've got a valid point there. I mean about the body, and it not being in the same place."

"Charlie, do you think Doug is dead, or that he ran off?"

He had to ponder that for a minute. From what he knew of Doug Lewison, he was a pampered, spoiled rich brat. That didn't say he was a killer. But from what Lyssa told him about his and Cathy Nunez's relationship, he was sadistic. It was his opinion that males with those tendencies got worse, not better, as they aged.

"Well, all I can say is that if he ran off, I hope he stays away from this area. If he is dead and buried somewhere, I can't think of anyone here in our town that will mourn him, except his parents. Lyssa, does that make me an awful person?"

"Charles Jason Koller, no it doesn't, not in my eyes. It means you are a person who doesn't want evil in his town, hurting the ones you love—that's all. Listen, my mom needs to use the phone. Talk tomorrow?"

"You can count on it. Hey, be careful riding with Libby tomorrow. She can be a handful on horseback."

"I will, and Charlie," she paused as her mom came into the room, giving her the signal to get off the phone. "I'm hanging up now, Mom. See you later, and, uh, you make me happy." She said the last words softly, breathed into the mouthpiece.

"You make me happy too, Lyssa. Bye." He cradled the phone.

"You gotta goofy face, bubba. Why don't you just tell her you love her?"

Charlie turned to find Libby sitting on the step down into the room.

"How long have you been eavesdropping, baby sister?" His tone sounded miffed, but the look on his face said he couldn't pull it off.

"You know, just like Josh Brolin's character in *The Goonies* says to his little brother Mikey: long enough, Charlie, long enough. I like Lyssa. No wait—I love her just like a sister. So, in a few years, you need to marry her and make her my real sister."

"Libby, I need your help in the kitchen," their mom called, so she hopped up and left Charlie sitting by himself.

Get married ... him and Lyssa?

Hmm, he thought, then wondered if small-town living was what she wanted and ranch life like he was planning. If they got married, she'd be living on land that was once owned by her family. How would that make her feel?

Funny, at twelve years old when he first met her, his heart had thudded in his ears, his mouth dried out, and his palms sweaty. Now, the thought of her not wanting a life with his, his heart thudded in his ears, his mouth grew dry, and his palms became sweaty.

The intense, overwhelming feeling of love—or the terrifying prospect of losing it—left him breathless.

29

AT 6: A.M. THE hallway phone rang. Libby Koller answered, stretching the extra-long cord to its limits, reaching over for the bowl of fresh fruit at the end of the long kitchen counter, plucking up a banana.

"Koller residence. Oh, hi, Lyssa. You on your way?"

"I gotta cancel, Libby. I'm sorry. Danny has the flu, and Mom doesn't want to leave him by himself. She's headed to Junction because she ran out of canning jars, then to work for half a day. So, it's either I stay here or drive to Junction. Either way, I can't meet you to ride fences today."

"No, I understand. Listen, don't worry—just help your mom out, and call me later this afternoon, or are you working?" She peeled the banana and took a tiny bite.

"I work tomorrow. Darn, a day off from Atticus Feed these days is rare. Can't believe I'll be stuck at home with a sick brother."

"Well, hey, we can ride another day, and this time for fun, not to hunt for fences that need mending."

"Deal. Tell Charlie I said 'morning.' Bye." Lyssa hung up, and as she turned to head back to the kitchen, an uneasy feeling settled in the pit of her stomach.

LINDY KOLLER PASSED HER daughter, smiled, and headed to the kitchen sink to finish up the dishes. She snatched up the igloo ice chest, took the sandwiches and a couple of apples from the fridge, and put them in, as well as individual bags of chips and some water. She filled a thermos with coffee, then tossed four granola bars into the cooler.

Paul crept up behind her, grabbed her, and kissed her neck.

"Lunches and my coffee ready to go?"

"Yep. Oh, and tell Charlie if he wants a soda to grab one from the mudroom—I never put them in the refrigerator."

"Charlie," his dad's voice carried. "Get a Coke from the mudroom."

Lindy Koller frowned. "Well, dang it, Paul, I could have screamed it. I wanted you to go tell him." She swatted at him, then shooed him away.

The red and green CF logo on Charlie's worn, red-and-white mesh hat—a relic from the trucking company, Consolidated Freight—settled with a gentle *plunk* onto his head as he walked into the room carrying a hot can of cola.

"Lyssa on her way?"

Libby relayed Lyssa's reasons for not going on the ride.

"Charlie, drop by later and see how Danny is? Ask Doris if she needs anything." Lindy wiped her hands on a worn dishtowel.

"Doris needs to get her a fella, then there'd be someone to help her out."

"Dad! Gosh, all women do not need a man! Geezers! If Mom was a single lady, she'd be fine."

This had Paul Koller raising his dark brown eyebrows. "Oh, do tell now, will you?"

"You know what I mean. You guys think us girls gotta have a man taking care of us."

Paul looked at Charlie, giving him the tiniest of winks, then he looked at his wife with fake concern. "You plan on being single sometime soon, Lindy? Because it'd be nice to know where I stand, and how many head of cattle I'll end up with and how much land."

"Well, I figure on keeping more than half..." Lindy began, but Libby rolled her eyes and threw a hand in the air. As she walked off, they heard her say, "Whatever, you guys."

The other three laughed.

———

MEN, BOYS, BROTHERS, AND dads.

The male population was bonkers if they thought women couldn't live without them. Sure, they were handy to have around, but girls were much more capable these days than they were, say, oh, one hundred years back.

No, strike that, thought Libby as she hooked the gate back and got onto Spunky, her light brown mare. Even back then, women had to be strong. Life was hard.

As she rode, checking the fence line, her thoughts went to the skeletons found and to the girl Cathy Nunez. She was only four years younger, and around six years younger than that girl Frannie when that all happened.

Libby shuddered at the thought of someone nab-
bing her, hurting or killing her, and then burying her
where no one could find her body. They'd found Frannie, but not Cathy, and her wild imagination went into
overdrive.

What if Cathy were buried on their ranch land and
she somehow uncovered her?

Would Cathy's killer come looking for her to keep it
a secret?

Her eyes went to a sagging pole.

Down off her mare, she tugged on work gloves,
got a roll of baling wire, wire cutters, and a piece of
plumbing pipe along with red tag tape. She wrapped
the wire around the pole, used the pipe to pull and
tighten it in a twisting motion, creating a temporary
repair, and affixed red tagging tape to mark the spot.

She'd note the pasture area in a notebook, then her
dad and brother would bring proper apparatuses and
supplies to fix the fence.

An uneventful riding-the-fence day was a fair
day—not much to be repaired on the back two hundred fifty acres. Libby had marked six spots: three sagging poles—easy fixes—and the others needed new
poles and re-wiring.

Old man Adair's land jutted up to a point at this
fence line, so she continued south past his property to
pick up the line to their back six hundred acres. This
was the land that had long ago been Red Oak Ranch,
owned by Lyssa's grandpa.

Funny thing about land boundaries.

Nothing was ever in a straight line, or a square turn.

The land that belonged to you might curve off one
way, then take off at a weird angle in a crooked line,

because things were never a perfect rectangle or circle when it came to the land and acreage.

The sloping hillsides presented a varied landscape, as larger mountains widened or narrowed at the base, while the waterways, in their unpredictable courses, flowed in any direction, changing the layout of the solid earth.

Libby Koller loved the outdoors, nature, and the pure energy it eluded. Her life on the land was all she'd known, and she thought about the people Mr. Adair said wanted to develop the land and create small towns of houses and communities.

She kicked her mare's flanks and galloped over grassy land, filled with tiny divots and curves, bumps, and dips. Her eyes ahead on the area of free-roaming land as her nostrils breathed in the clean country air.

No smog, no car fumes, no noisy traffic; just peace and tranquility.

They had moved half of their cattle up to the northern green pasture to graze for the next forty days and the other half to the east pasture.

Pop had over-seeded the south meadow with rye grass and, in forty days, he'd move half the herd there into the divided paddocks.

This fence check was important because Paul and Charlie were about to put up more fence lines to divide the larger area into smaller grazing paddocks.

What if a developer wanted her dad to sell out? Would he do it if the money was right?

Libby, eyes closed, slowed Spunky to a walk, running her fingers through the horse's soft, silken mane.

She tried to envision this area filled with houses and roads, schools, apartments, gas stations, and every type of store, from grocer to clothing or five-and-dime.

No clean air or wide-open spaces.

No stars at night.

No yipping or howling of a pack of coyotes.

Stock tanks filled in, and no more skinny-dipping.

No mountains or hillsides filled with wildflowers.

How awful that sounded.

Out here in the natural land, you'd find lizards and snakes, rats, bugs, rabbits, wolves, and coyotes, along with buzzard hawks and owls. Dangerous, yes, if you tangled with the wrong wildlife. But bringing in more people? More dangerous.

The world was full of meanness.

Humans like Doug Lewison or the few bullies she'd encountered at school—and yes, even small towns had their share—were a cancer that ate at any place they lay their head.

Libby sighed. So just when the heck had she become an advocate for staying true to your country roots?

A giggle bubbled up. She so wished Lyssa had been on this ride. They could have talked about next year being her senior year, plans for the future, and a prom dress debacle that was bound to happen since she wasn't much of a dress-wearing sort.

Libby pulled on the reins to stop the mare.

She gazed around, taking in the area.

Heavens to Betsy, she was off course.

Where was her head?

She knew ... in the darned clouds, of course. She had passed old man Adair's fence line and was now riding the backside of the Lewison's property—the parcel that met the county's unincorporated road, one no one ever used.

Everyone figured one day in the future they'd build a superhighway to get from Hotspur to Mexico in one direction and to Louisiana in the other.

A man was digging by the fence, and at first she wasn't sure who, but as she came close, she saw it was Harry Grist, the hired help of the snotty rich Lewisons.

Libby was a congenial gal, and it wouldn't hurt to chat a minute ... or so she thought.

Her hand lifted in a wave as she called, "Woo hoo, Mr. Grist, I'm riding over!"

Grist's head shot up, and the shovel he was wielding stopped mid-air.

The man had not been expecting company.

30

LIBBY WALKED THE MARE up to the barbed-wire fence and looked down at Harry Grist, who was patting dirt into a fresh hole. She tried to keep her face from scrunching into a confused expression, wondering why he'd dug a hole only to fill it back in.

What was he doing—burying something? A dead animal? Treasure?

"Hiya, Mr. Grist. Didn't expect to see anyone out this far."

"Miss Libby, why are you out this far yourself?"

"Oh, uh, I was riding our fences for my dad today and, well, got inside my own thoughts and let Spunky here wander, I guess."

She patted the mare's neck, her hands trembling a little. "So... what are you burying?"

"Burying?" Grist scowled, then looked down at the overturned ground and the shovel. "Oh, I was, uh—gonna add a fence post here, but decided not to."

Libby glanced over the man's shoulder, looking for a new post, posthole diggers, wire cutters, or wire clips. No post. No tools. There was just him, work gloves, a shovel, and on the ground, an empty canvas bag.

"Okay, well, I'll leave you to your work. I've got to head back."

Harry lifted the shovel, and she flinched, pulling the reins to walk the mare backward. The look on her face startled him.

"What's the matter, Miss Libby?" he asked, his voice low. "You afraid of me?"

"No, sir. I just need to get back to my duties. I missed the last mile of fence back yonder," she said, turning her mare to leave.

"Hey—did you ever meet the Lewisons' son, Doug?"

The off-the-cuff question felt odd to the young girl.

"No. He was much older than me. Him and my brothers weren't friends. Why do you ask?" Curiosity stirred, and she pulled the reins tighter to keep Spunky still. Libby's mare had a tendency to feel her emotions; they'd bonded soon after the horse was born.

"Just asking, I suppose. Your brother Charlie was close to Marlin's age, I reckon. Marlin was a decent kid—nice, funny, and a little lost. I miss that boy, and knowing it was his bones they found makes me sick to my stomach, thinking about what might've happened to that kid on that old man's land."

The sudden urge to defend Gus rose, her spine bristling.

"Mr. Adair would never harm a child—ever! How can you even say that out loud? Maybe that boy— that douche bag—Doug, or even his dad, did it. That runaway was living with you, though, wasn't he?"

Harry Grist tossed the shovel to the ground and wiped his face with a rag from his back pocket.

"I cared about that boy. Wanted him to stay here with me." He looked up at Libby, sadness etched across his face.

"The Lewisons' son was cruel—I grant you that—and his folks are odd, too. But they're my paycheck. That rich, snotty boy was a lot of grief, and he was never nice to Marlin. Shoot, Doug was nasty to his mom, too, but you don't need to repeat any of this, uh..." He stumbled over his words.

"With him gone, don't do any good to talk bad about a person. I reckon I need to get back to my chores."

Without a goodbye, Harry trotted off to where he'd parked the old beat-up ranch truck, cranked it, and pulled away, the truck rattling and bumping across the hard pastureland.

She watched him drive until all she could see was a flash of bumper as sunlight reflected off it.

Libby, being a smart girl, caught the past-tense references. *Was* cruel. *Was* a lot of grief. *Was* never nice to Marlin. *Was* nasty to his mom.

Was.

Harry Grist's words sounded final. Not that Doug was missing and might come back.

Libby heard the unspoken message: Doug was dead.

But by whose hand?

Had Harry killed him? Had he also killed Cathy? And what was Harry doing out here, digging?

Back on Koller ranch land, she finished the rear fence line and decided it was too hot to continue. That—and she'd wasted time wandering and chatting with Mr. Grist.

She'd start over early the next morning, in cooler weather, and finish up. Few repairs were needed so far, which was fantastic news for her father.

Still, her mind drifted back to Grist, the shovel, and the hole he'd filled.

He had buried something.

A chill crept up her spine... or someone.

No, she told herself. Her imagination was getting away from her. She'd keep this to herself, then come back later with a shovel and find out what it was.

Dead animals wouldn't faze her. Years of country life had exposed her to the sight and smell of dead cattle, calves, wolves, and rabbits—a grim but common occurrence.

But if it wasn't one of those things...

A cold sweat slicked her palms. Her heart hammered against her ribs, changing everything.

THREE-THIRTY THE NEXT MORNING Charlie found his little sister eating a bowl of cold cereal at the kitchen table.

"Why are you up so early, Lib?" Charlie poured himself a glass of orange juice, popped two pieces of bread into the toaster, and pushed the plunger. "You want toast?"

He didn't wait for her answer.

"No, no toast, thanks. I gotta ride the rest of the fences, and, um, wanted an early start. I wanna recheck the south pasture too—the fence line that ends at the Lewisons', next to that corner by Mr. Adair's place. Yesterday I thought I noticed a few sagging posts, so I wanted to check them out for the old man."

The toast popped up. Charlie grabbed it, plopped it on a plate, slathered it with butter, then added grape jam. He frowned.

Without looking at her, he asked, "Why were you that far south, Lib? That ain't near our fenced pastures."

"Seems my head went a-wandering. I free-reined Spunky, let her go where her legs took her, and I went along with my head in the clouds."

"Little sister, one day you're gonna get in a world of hurt 'cause you aren't paying attention. If I were you, I'd steer clear of the Lewisons' property, too."

"Why? Is it because you think they had something to do with those skeletons and that bundle of clothes you found?"

Mouth full of jelly-toast, he swallowed and wiped his lips. "Well, it does seem kinda odd, and they don't seem too worried about their son, so that's stranger still. If your kinfolk wasn't in contact and you couldn't find them, wouldn't you be worried?"

"I guess. Especially if it was my kid. But their son was mean, so what if he was mean to them too, and they—" Libby stopped. She couldn't say it.

"You saying they killed their own boy?" He stared at her. "Gawd almighty, Elizabeth Lorrine Koller! Don't say that to anyone outside this family. You start gossip like that and all hell might break loose. Let Chief Grayson handle the accusations and all that."

"I wasn't gossiping, Charlie. I was just talking to *you*. And don't call me by my full name again—you know I don't like it."

"Well, stay off their land. I heard in town they're trying to get back to California and can't wait to leave this hot, backward state."

Libby rinsed her empty bowl at the sink, her face tight with an intense frown when she looked over at him.

"Charlie?"

"Mm?"

"If I never came home... would you come looking for me?"

The question—and her tone—startled him.

"Why, lordy, Lib, of course I would. You're my only sister. And, well, Mom and Dad would kick my ass if I didn't."

"Gee, thanks. Only 'cause Mom and Dad would be mad?" She huffed.

He stepped beside her, slipped an arm around her shoulders, and gave her a squeeze. "Nah. I'd hunt for you because I love you, baby sister, and it'd break my heart if something happened to you."

"Aww, Charlie Brown. I love you too, you big lummox."

She tiptoed up and kissed his cheek. "Tell Mom I did my chores and that I'm gone. I should be back after one. See you later."

He watched her bound out the back door carrying a bag of bottled water, knowing she'd packed two granola bars and bagged peanuts too—just in case.

At first, he smiled.

Then a faint crease formed at the corner of his eyes.

His sister... he hoped she wasn't playing detective with the Lewisons.

31

LIBBY FED HER MOM'S chickens and refilled the watering troughs. Next, she switched on the three soaker hoses in her mother's garden and set the homemade timer for thirty minutes. She was ready to saddle Spunky and head out less than forty minutes later.

After leading the horse out, she closed the barn door, mounted, and aimed her mare to the south pasture. At the gate, she slipped off, lifted the chain, pushed it open, led the horse out, then reattached it, securing the closure.

Back on her steed, she nudged Spunky forward at a steady walk, then angled her head backward to see her family home. Her mom would be up by now, coffee percolating as she fried bacon and scrambled eggs for her dad's breakfast.

Charlie would have already told her where she was headed, and Libby wondered if he would also voice his unease about what he thought she was up to.

"Charlie you worry too much," their mother would say, adding that Libby was strong-willed and independent. Lindy Koller's smile would have an edge of pride and concern.

Libby was her only daughter, and she had raised her to be independent; however, it was her spirited independence that also caused her mom's concern.

Today, though, Charlie did not voice his thoughts and hoped it was the right decision.

———

THE SUN WASN'T UP, but had peeked over the hillside, shining orange and yellowish rays over the short brown grasses and weeds of the south pasture.

Libby looked up and the stars were twinkling; a sight she would never tire of. Dark bluish-gray skies intertwined with streaks of thin white clouds which were slow moving and few. The many patterns of stars glittered and scattered across the early morning sky.

She inhaled.

The smells of dirt and hay, and in the wind, wafted the scent of Koller's cattle not too far off and the distinct smells of Mr. Adair's goats.

Her entire body relaxed as she laid her hands atop the saddle horn, and her fingers held the reins. This was paradise for Elizabeth Lorrine Koller; or as she most adamantly preferred to be called Libby.

Her face pinched in a narrowed scowl.

What if she were to find that a boy's body was buried where Harry Grist was digging?

She liked Mr. Grist, sort of anyway.

Gus Adair was her favorite older person, and she had never feared him.

Harry Grist was younger, but there was something less friendly regarding him.

Adair was talkative and had a smile. He laughed and joked; and was a genuine person with a heart.

Harry walked around with a sour expression and gave off vibes of being antisocial.

What did she even know about the man, Harry Grist?

Had he been married, did he ever have kids?

Libby felt bad for judging the man on his looks alone. Maybe his life had been hard and sad. Who knew?

What had Charlie said after that bundle of clothes was found?

Hadn't Grist got distraught and upset, crying out that runaway boy's name?

Libby scolded herself for judging a person without giving them the benefit of the doubt; the only thing was, what if she gave him the benefit of the doubt and then had herself caught up in something sinister, or life threatening?

Ghost stories and thriller flicks flashed in her head. *Children of The Corn, Pet Sematray, and Stepfather...* all scary movies.

Libby shuddered.

She did not want to be living in a real-life horror show.

Libby focused on the land ahead of her and shook these creepy ideas from her head.

The land—the sky—the air.

If what Mr. Adair said came true, then others like the Lewison family would move here and crowd the place; bring in a new way of living and advancement to ruin the area and push them out.

She hoped it would never affect her or her family. She hoped it wouldn't disrupt their peaceful life in the fresh country air.

Progress to her was more cattle and chickens, a bigger barn or her father getting a pasture irrigation system in place in every paddock. Six more bulls and more calving in the summer. Not more houses; more buildings and smog from more traffic.

Libby Koller was and would remain a country gal her whole life.

The sun lit up the sky as it rose higher, and Libby grabbed her sunglasses and plunked them on, then pulled up her hat and covered her head. It was supposed to be a scorcher today.

In the distance she saw the fence line of the Lewison's, and a man's figure hunched over.

Libby reined in her horse, took a big breath, held it, and let it out.

She was riding an animal that was faster than stepping on the gas pedal and going from zero to sixty in a minute—Spunky could move if she felt like it. With a nudge from both heels into her ride's flanks, she moved forward, and Spunky snorted, and the man looked up.

It wasn't Mr. Grist, but Art Lewison.

He straightened to look at her, holding a single dirty brick in his right hand.

Libby watched him. His old, unshaven face cycled through several expressions, beginning with sadness, moving to startled, and morphing into an angry fear.

"Young lady. What are you doing out here? You do know you are on private property, right?" His body rigid: his words clipped.

"I, uh, was riding my father's fences yesterday and noticed some of Mr. Adair's post were sagging. They connect to your line, and I came to recheck them for the old fella." Libby lied, something she wasn't very good at.

"He can check his own fences. He has before. The man is not incapable. You need to leave, and you'd best not be on my property again, or I'll speak with the auth, uh, your parents."

Libby heard his misstep.

She felt sure he was just about to say "authorities".

She lowered her eyes to the top of the saddle horn, her gaze glancing down to the edge of the fence line; and knew this was where Harry Grist had been digging the day before.

That was when she noticed three reddish brown bricks pushed into the soft earth, and a few more laying there alongside a garden hoe.

She didn't or couldn't help herself as her lips formed the words that popped out before she thought about what she was saying.

"Are you marking a grave?"

His eyes widened, his mouth dropped open, and his body went stiff, and his tone just contained.

"What did you just ask me, girl?"

Libby's fingers tightened around the reins, and her heart thudded, but she was braver than she looked.

"Is that a grave, Mr. Lewison? Is this where your son is buried?"

Art stood stiff, then the hand holding the brick moved, and Libby narrowed her eyes at the man.

Was he gonna try tossing that at her?

She stared him down, almost daring him.

"You, girl, are out of line. It would be in your best interest to leave and not be gossiping about me and my family. Do I make myself clear?"

"Be in the best interest of our community to find out the truth and for people like you to pay for your sins, and ..."

That was all she got out before the brick hit her at a glancing blow hard enough to send her off the other side of her horse, and for the mare to bolt when the second block hit her in the flank.

Art, old as he was, was still agile and he made it over the barbed wire, ripping his pants, and putting a gash in his lower calf.

He jerked Libby up, shaking her and screaming.

He'd had enough of everything, and this had been his breaking point.

Blood trickled from her temple, and he stopped screaming when he saw the ooze of warm red liquid, and he let her body drop to the ground.

Libby's gaze went to where her horse had been standing and watched Spunky hightailing it off, and she knew the mare knew her way back to the ranch.

After that, it went dark.

Art pulled the kerchief from his back pocket and dabbed at her gash.

Not deep, but it hit her hard enough to knock her out, or she hit her head when she fell. He wasn't sure of which. All he was certain of was now he had just made matters worse.

His resentment of Camille; his dislike of the boy he called son, and his hatred of this hot hillbilly state.

Then the girl, the one that had seduced him right under his wife's nose and had then played him for a fool.

32

He carried her as far as he could, then had to stop.

Damn, why had he parked the jeep so far away?

For a slip of a girl, she was heavy dead weight, heavier than the others had been.

Others. He might need a tally sheet.

What the hell was he going to do?

This Koller girl would be a big deal in this town; not like that Swisher kid, or even Cathy Nunez, the girl Doug brought home. That story was explainable because she had fancied Doug first; and this had been an easier story to concoct.

Sure, Doug was no angel, not after the Missy Van de Bern incident; Art was sure of the boy's guilt.

His memories of seeing what Doug once did to a poor cat were disturbing, but he'd held his tongue.

Art knew if he were the reason Doug was stripped from their lives, Camille would toss him out.

If that happened, he would be a penniless vagrant on the dirtier streets of San Francisco.

It was her family money ... her wealth, not his.

He had nothing until he met and wooed her.

What he lacked was financial control. She was easy to manipulate in love; but the woman's fingers were clasped to the purse strings in a death hold.

About to hoist the limp girl back up, she stirred, moaning.

Not good.

Art put the kerchief around her mouth and tied it tight. Then he pulled his belt off and, twisting her arms to her back, looped the strap through the buckle several times until he could push the bar in and over the prong.

He used Libby's belt to fasten her feet together to keep her from running.

It was the best he could do without having duct tape or zip ties.

Her vision—blurry, she blinked, focusing in on him, and he saw the questions in her eyes.

"It's a long story, not sure we have the time," he said.

In one swift move, Art hoisted her up and over his shoulder.

"Be still and don't fight me. I won't harm you, but I need to think, and I don't need anybody to see me and you out here, so I gotta get you back to the house."

After depositing her into the front seat of the jeep, he cranked it up and took off for the back of the house, next to the freestanding three-car garage.

Art huffed and puffed and got her out of the jeep, taking her through the mudroom, down to the cellar.

Libby's face, smudged with dirt; blood dried on her temple and cheek.

He fastened her ankle to a hook at the far end of the cellar and attached it with a chain. Then he looped it on the bottom shelf of an empty wine rack—fixing her hands behind her with a zip tie.

He gave her a drink of water and re-taped her mouth shut.

He put his belt back on.

"I'll be back later to check on you."

It was all he said as he left her in the dank, musty cellar.

She watched as his foot disappeared and the door shut out the light; a tear fell from her eye, then another.

Art looked at the gash on his leg and grimaced.

In his dressing room, he cleaned the wound, changed his trousers, tossing the torn ones in a hamper.

He knew Camille would sleep until noon, and Harry Grist wasn't to be there until ten to pack up the attic, then work his way downstairs, packing what he could in a day's time.

It was 8 am, and he damn well needed a stiff drink, maybe a few.

Two drinks relaxed him.

His mind wandered as he sat in the den, his third drink in hand, but not drinking.

He closed his eyes ... his past came alive.

The things he'd done he could not undo, and now he feared his sins were coming back, not to haunt him but to destroy him.

Those years ago, if he'd just reported what he knew, there would be no fingers to point at him.

Art raised the glass to his lips; he had to stay lucid, so he sipped, he did not gulp.

It had been when the runaway showed up, and Art saw Doug's reactions to the camaraderie between Harry and the boy.

The hate radiated from Doug for something he had envied: a closeness to a father figure.

Art understood why Doug had picked Ryan Chapin, a poor kid from the other side of the tracks, as his best friend.

Envy.

Doug wanted what Ryan had. Ryan's dad treated Doug like a son.

Harry had taken a liking to Marlin and an instant dislike of Doug, which was Camille's fault for acting so damned snooty and treating Grist like a dirty servant.

His mind flashed back to that night.

By the time he'd been able to locate Doug, the boy Marlin was almost dead; there was nothing he could do about it.

But he stayed and watched, then followed.

He had to admit he admired Doug's plan at the disposal of the body, which was what gave him the idea for the Swisher kid's corpse.

Damn the boy, though. If not for Doug's night-time activities, his own dark doorway would not have re-opened.

And for these demons to be brought back to life in such a small, backwards town, making it impossible not to be caught, not like in a sprawling place like San Francisco.

He took another sip, set the glass down, licked his lips, and the face of Cathy Nunez floated in his head.

Pretty little minx.

At first he ignored her, but as time had gone on, it had been hard not to.

She and Doug flaunted their relationship in front of him and his mother. It had pleased Camille her son had a girl.

That stupid girl thought it was him who was rich.

Cathy had cornered him one night and said she would run off with him if he promised to help her parents get out of financial debt.

Enraged by her coaxing and flirtatious behavior, losing control after she laughed at his failed advances, Art had not been able to stop, and he had choked the life from her.

It flashed back—in living color.

"You stupid little girl, look what you've made me do?"

His face twisted in an ugly sneer as she lay on the barn floor.

Just as fast, that anger turned into remorse, and he kneeled to see if she might still have a pulse.

No.

Dead.

She was dead.

He stood, paced, fretted. Then he heard a noise. Someone was headed to the barn; they were whistling.

Damn it.

It was Harry Grist; he had to hide the body.

With speed and strength his pumping adrenaline afforded him, he lifted her body, placing it between bales of hay, pushing up loose hay over the end, and making sure her feet were covered.

The doors squealed open; the bottom scraping the wood plank flooring, and Harry stopped whistling when he saw Art.

"Mr. Lewison? What are you doing out here at this time of night?"

Lewison ignored the question, firing back one of his own. "Mr. Grist, you are still on property?"

"Oh, yes, sir. I hadn't cleaned out the horse stalls yet or put in new hay. Ran behind today with the extra chores your Mrs. asked me to do."

Camille was always messing his life up.

Art felt trapped.

What reason could he provide for Harry not to do his job; then it hit him.

"I have a tremendous problem, Mr. Grist, and sure could use your help, and your discretion..." he paused, then added, "and I will make it well worth your while."

That night, Art learned Harry Grist was swayed by money, and his silence could be bought.

He'd also learned two other things about his hired help.

One: Grist had a few arrests on his record; nothing violent; but stuff he'd rather keep hushed in Hotspur. (Stalking and robbery.)

Two: the man was gullible and believed Art was covering for his son's accident to protect both the boy and his mother.

Art was not Doug's father, and never one day in his life had he loved Camille Harris Lewison; just her money and the lifestyle it bought him.

Plus, with Doug gone, he'd be her only living heir.

33

"TIFF, DID YOU GET the mail from the PO box today?"

"Oh, shoot, no. I'll go now, be back in a jiff, Chief."

At his desk, he ran a hand down his face. He was tired and frustrated. The developers were on his back, the surveyors—dragging their feet, as he had requested—and his brother had called, updating him on the counter actions the home builders were taking to complete the land sale and start the groundwork for the new housing development.

Thank goodness Glen Adair had also put his own kink in the mix.

He had hired an outside attorney to assist him with farm zoning so no one could complain about his goats, the smells, or the noise. His idea was to build a brick structure high enough to not see his property from the boundaries of the new planned community.

Toby closed his eyes and his thoughts when back to a recent meeting of the three towns they'd gathered for at the Auction House in Link two weeks ago.

These men were all smart, honest men who had never shirked a day of work and cared about their community.

Growth was a worry for these people because a certain expansion to them was dangerous. Toby understood. If their town's population increased, so would the need for more police watching out for unsavory types.

Yep. It made perfect sense to him.

A larger bustling city increased the likelihood of attracting more malicious individuals.

He kept it to himself, but in his head, he was thinking about Art and Camille and all that had happened in Hotspur since they arrived seven years back.

Since then, two bodies were found; two were still missing, and Toby felt it was his mission to help his small town heal by finding out the truth and then moving forward from there.

Tiff broke him out of his reveries. "Here, Chief, got a passel of mail, including junk." She lay the stack on his desk. "I took out the bills and will go over them with Marge, so we can get them paid."

"Thanks, Tiff, shut my door will you?"

After his door shut, Toby gave a long hard stretch over his head and yawned, drained the lukewarm coffee left in his stained NYPD souvenir coffee cup, and grabbed the mail.

His process was to separate mail by size, so he picked up the stack and straightened it as the smaller pieces fell to the bottom, and all he held were larger envelopes, magazines, sales papers, and whatnot. He sat it down on his right, stacked up all the other parcels and set that bunch at the far-left top corner of his desk then turned his attention to the larger envelopes when the return address on one caught his eye. LAPD Los Altos, CA.

His heart pounded; had the detective come through for him?

He slit open the envelope and pulled out the sheaf of pages. A sticky note was on top.

'Grayson, you were right. Art Lewison had a record, con artist, robbery, and assault. All juvvie charges that were dismissed, and he was never charged officially. Seems his grandmother had friends. One wasn't dismissed though, and it was never expunged; but sealed. I had to ask a lot of favors for this, so use it wisely.' M. Gonzales.

Toby looked over the report; a large gasp sounded as he read.

July1955; thirty-eight years ago. On the campus of Massachusetts State College, the body of a girl was found in the water near the Harbor Walk Road; her clothing snagged on the rocks.

She was identified as twenty-three-year-old Wanda Elaine Roberts from Dorchester. She lived in the dormitories with two roommates.

Toby read on to find that there had been a weekend bash that had lasted well into the morning hours. New graduates from high school enrolled to start at the university in the fall; along with returning second and third-year students were in attendance.

Arthur David Lewison, 19, a new freshman, was there with his best friend, Patrick Murphy, a sophomore.

Toby saw another sticky note handwritten from Detective Gonzales.

I checked out this Patrick Murphy, too. He died three years ago in a one car auto accident with a blood alcohol level of 0.12. Before that, though, he had an impressive criminal history, as well. Assault, burglary, and drug possession; he was named but not charged in two murders; and did a four-year stint for aggravated assault with a deadly weapon on a former girlfriend.'

"Hmm," Toby's voice very low, "you had some dis-reputable friends did you, Art? Did they get away with murder? Did you?"

Toby flipped to the next page.

The murder of Wanda Roberts happened in late July, and if they hadn't found her body when they had, she might never have been found. That same year, the next month, in August, Hurricane Connie blew in. Five days later, Hurricane Diane followed.

The body of 23-year-old Wanda Roberts would have been lost forever; and her case would be that of a missing woman, not an unsolved homicide.

This was interesting, but where did Art Lewison fit in?

He continued to read.

Ah ... there it was—the connection he'd been looking for.

One of the deceased roommates told the police that Art knew Wanda through Patrick; she was a math tu-tor, and Patrick had been failing calculus until he met her and then they started dating.

He read the interviews:

"Art had an insatiable need to get Wanda's attention," the roommate named Georgia said. *"He followed Patrick like a piece of chewing gum stuck to his shoe, because of Wanda. I think he even snuck into the bedroom when Pat and Wanda were, uh, you know, doing it, so he could watch."*

"Yeah, and I think Patrick let him watch," the second roommate, Clarie, declared with wide eyes. *"Patrick was creepy, too. He was a flirt, and not very subtle about it either."*

"It was at that party though," Georgia said, *"things got heated, and the three of them got into a huge argument,*

screaming loud, and it disrupted the fun. I remember a guy, uh, Kenny Manchester, and he asked them to leave. They were all drunk and Patrick took a swing at Kenny and missed, and then Kenny punched him in the stomach."

Toby read Claire's statement: Wanda got upset, helped Patrick up, asked Art to help her, and then they left. It was 1:00 A.M.

That had been the last anyone had seen of the three; except one person made a comment that he saw Patrick, who was lying passed out on a bench by the cafeteria doors at two a.m., because he had to pass that way to get to his dorm.

No one knew where Art was, and when questioned by the police, he denied staying with Patrick and Wanda and he'd gone straight home.

There was no one to corroborate his story; and there was one person who could put Patrick in a place far from where Wanda's body had been dumped.

There was a lot of conjecture that made sense, however no eyewitnesses and no physical proof.

The police interrogation:

Officer Mallory: "Mr. Lewison, may I call you Art?"

Toby read the question-and-answer report taken back then. He could almost hear the flat monotone answers from a boy who had no conscience or heart.

He sat back when he was done.

Hadn't Sergeant Detective Manny Gonzales said something similar about Doug's cross-examination regarding Missy Van de Bern? The boy was soulless; and even though not related to him through blood, Art displayed the same sick attitude.

He let out a sad sigh from his slightly closed lips.

Children learn from their environment and their up-bringing.

Doug learned haughtiness and entitlement from Camille; and from Art he learned about unkindness and cruelty. Art may not have directly imparted these ideals to Doug, but their essence quietly infiltrated his being, shaping his innermost thoughts.

Art.

Toby straightened.

He was now a person of interest; and he had to speak with him, only the man would not let him pass the front door; nor was he going to come to this, as he'd called it, rinky-dink police office, either.

34

HIS DAY BEGAN FAR too early—5:00 a.m.

First a trip to the burial site of the girl, a location Grist selected. Next a visit to where Harry transferred his nephew's skeletal remains.

There was no reasonable justification for him being there. Just to think, he decided.

Two and a half glasses of bourbon later, he was relaxed enough to close his eyes and fall asleep.

Disoriented, he heard a man's voice down the hall and wiped the alcohol cobwebs from his eyes.

It was Grist.

His heart raced—then calmed.

He wouldn't go into the cellar, no need to.

Neither would Camille, because the wine was packed away and now spiders and dirt would keep her out.

"Mr. Lewison, you back there?"

"In the den, Grist."

Harry stepped in, hat in his hands, a concerned look on his face.

"You drive the jeep somewhere, sir?"

He set his empty glass down.

Art's tone brusque.

"If I did, you think it's your business?"

"Well, no sir, guess not."

Harry tried to contain his own anger; this man had asked a lot of him and should be treating him better.

"Don't go upstairs. My wife is still sleeping, and I don't want her disturbed. Go to the garage and start sorting through the mechanical tools, and the tool-boxes. Keep the tools you want, for free. Sort out the few I might need to do handy work on a small home."

Art waved him off.

A grimace crossed Harry's face.

Free tools—another payoff for keeping his mouth shut.

For a split second he thought about calling the Chief of Police and telling him everything; but then he'd get implicated in a coverup.

He didn't commit the murders, so how much time would he have to serve?

How had he gotten himself into this mess?

He should have high-tailed it to Toby and spilled what he knew—fact was—he knew the truth.

Once Harry was out of the house, Art went to the cellar to check on the girl.

Her eyes opened at the sound of his steps.

He stared at her.

There was no way out of this unless he kept her hidden here.

If he didn't feed her, she would die, and he needed to let her have her 'personal time'.

A bucket and washcloths.

Yeah, he'd do that, or ... what was one more body?

He'd killed four people now, and this Libby girl would make five.

Damn it.

It wasn't like he'd wanted to kill any of them; he wasn't a serial killer—on purpose.

In a kaleidoscope of memories, he re-lived his past, beginning with his first encounter with death in the late summer of 1955.

***

Wanda.

If she had just let him kiss her that night and not laughed and pushed him away, calling him a loser kid.

His anger had blinded him and when he got his vision back, he'd found himself hunkered over her limp body, his hands still around her neck.

As his adrenaline rush slowed and his breathing evened out, he sat on her chest, looking at her face.

Her eyes wide open, lifeless, yet still pretty to him.

With the back of his hand, he caressed her yet still warm cheek and pushed her wavy dark hair back behind her ear.

She could never call him loser again, so he kissed her dead lips, and lay over her, like a lover would after making love, and he hugged her.

It had been very nice, until the dreaming Art woke, and panicked.

Her carcass was small, but heavy.

What was it with dead weight?

He'd tossed Wanda into the Savin Hill Cove, hoping for her corpse to get carried out of the channel into the ocean.

The Swisher kid.

He had made a serious blunder.

She was tall and more advanced for her age, and he'd thought she was the woman who was cheating on her husband with her brother-in-law from Idaho.

It had been too late to just say, "Oops, wrong girl."

Cathy, with her flirting and then refusal had pressed similar buttons likened to those of Wanda Roberts.

And just like that night in Boston, the irate monster rose.

It happened fast and in a dream state. Only Grist's appearance had shaken him from his trance and spurred his fear.

Doug.

Now that he enjoyed, wanting to kill him; and the boy did not have to give him any provocation. Well, not really.

He'd heard Doug and Camille discuss his arrangement with Cathy, and how, if he had a girl to take back to California, it would be best.

She was a sweet girl who doted on him, and he needed that in his life, since he'd never found it until she came along.

"Call her, better yet," Camille advised, "go get her, bring her back, tell her you made a mistake, and you want her to go to San Antonio with you, then when you get her here you can explain California."

"Mom, I was kinda mean to her, not just the other day, but other times."

"Get her a present, Dougie, or wait," Camille clapped her hands.

"Tell her you are getting your trust fund early and you and her can buy a house and you can send her to college in San Francisco."

Doug had puckered his brows.

Was his mother playing games with him?

Once he knew she was serious, he would do it, knowing he could dump the stupid kid later, after the dust settled and the ink was dry on the paperwork.

Art had been there, his teeth grinding, his hatred of both Camille and Doug festering like a boil in his armpit.

His inner monster grinned, though.

He and Doug needed a bonding moment, and he knew how to get that damn kid's attention, and how to draw him in.

***

"Doug, got a minute?"

"What, Dad? I'm going into Hotspur, don't have a lot of time."

"Won't take too long. Meet me at the jeep."

Art was in the driver's seat.

"Get in, wanna show you something important before you go," he paused, then said "please, son," then forced a smile.

"Alright, I guess I have a little time. I mean it's not like Cathy's going to run off anywhere, right?"

He jumped into the passenger side.

"Nah, she's gonna stay put, wherever she is."

Doug was oblivious to his adoptive father's sinister smile as his foot pressed the accelerator.

They drove and the jeep turned onto the road that ended at Gus Adair's fence line, same road he'd lured Marlin too, a lump formed in Doug's throat.

What sort of game was his father playing at?

"I saw you that night, Doug. That poor boy."

Doug moved to get out of the jeep, but Art reached out, grabbing his wrist. For an old man, he was strong, and the boy looked at his hand, then at his face.

"Dad, let go of my wrist."

"If I were your dad, I would, but I'm not."

The timbre of his voice startled Doug, and his body relaxed in surprise, giving Art the upper hand to get a deeper hold on the boy, snatching his wrist and snapping a zip tie on it, then connecting it to the wide steering wheel.

"What the ... hey, what are you doing and what do you mean if you were my dad, dad?"

"You tortured that boy, just like you did that cat you stole from the Jacob's house. I watched you and it horrified me, both the feline and the kid."

"You're my dad. How can you say things like that to me?"

Doug pulled on the skinny plastic tie, and Art swatted his hand away, then he slapped the boy across the face.

"Shut up. I am not your father. I am your non-blood-related uncle you stupid twit. Your parents are dead. Your mother killed your father then herself because they were both crazy, schizophrenic loony-tunes."

Doug's mouth fell open—his eyes narrowed in disbelief.

"That can't be. You mean my mom is my aunt?"

Art explained it, rather he paraphrased it as he got out and zip tied the other arm to the handle of the door, then released the zip tie from the steering wheel.

"Why—why not tell me? I don't understand?"

Art reached into the back and grabbed a metal bar from the floorboard.

"Because, my dear boy, your aunt could not have kids. This was her one chance to be a mother, and she would not have it destroyed by you knowing the truth. Now, get out, and stand up," Art instructed, as he stepped back brandishing the heavy bar.

Doug fought back, with his entire body, feet, and legs kicking, his one free arm swiping and punching at this man—who was now a stranger to him.

His fear intensified, and he understood what his victims must have experienced.

This man would kill him, but not without a fight.

One kick landed in Art's knee, and he faltered backward, and a snarling laugh spurted.

"I've given you more leeway than you gave any of your victims, boy, especially all the innocent animals."

"You won't get away with this because my mom, and *she is* my mom, she'll come looking for me."

"She might, but when Camille thinks you ran off with the girl and didn't consider her feelings, she'll be sad then angry. I will be there to console her and tell her you were just like her sister, your schizoid mother, and you can't be trusted."

"Cathy will come back. She'll be worried, and she'll look for me, too."

Doug was sure she would. The girl loved him even with the crap he'd put her through and made her do. Cathy Nunez was obsessed with him and the money he would come into one day.

"Nope, that won't happen foolish boy, not unless she can uncover herself from the grave she now lives in."

Doug's eyes stretched open and his mouth gaped with an inhaled sharp gasp.

"She's dead? You killed Cathy, too?"

With a raise of his forehead, his brows moving up, his head tilted as an evil gleam settled in his eyes, Art shrugged, then raised the crowbar and bashed Doug's skull.

Rendered unconscious—Doug's body hung, pulling his shoulder out of its socket. He dangled above the ground.

Choking an unconscious person didn't seem like a lot of fun, so Art gave his head another bash, waited for a three second beat, then felt for a pulse.

Dead.

Good.

He'd already dug a shallow grave for the boy, and with Grist's help later, he'd moved the body to the cellar.

Re-living these moments took him under two minutes.

He returned to the question he needed an answer to: how to handle Libby Koller?

35

PAUL STOPPED THE TRUCK, his tires digging into the soft earth.

"Charlie, what the heck is Spunky doing in that field?"

Charlie followed his father's finger and sat straighter.

"Unless that mare got close to a rattler and bolted, Libby would never have fallen off, Dad."

Charlie hesitated.

Did he want to spill his thoughts about his little sister's adventure—or had the horse just gotten spooked and bucked her off?

Paul jumped out, followed by Charlie, as they ran to the mare. His gloved hands grabbed the two-strand barbed wire at the top, and he hauled himself over the mesh fencing, his son on his heels.

Spunky stood still, knowing both men, and she neighed.

"Spunk, it's okay. Take it easy, girl."

Charlie grabbed her reins, patting her muscular neck.

"Where's Libby?" a question the horse couldn't answer, but she snorted when she heard the name.

Paul looked the animal over, then his gaze swept across the flat land of the pasture.

"The mare isn't injured. You talked to Lib this morning before she left?" he asked, looking back at his son.

"Yeah. She said she was heading to the south pasture where our land, Adair's, and the Lewisons meet at that one corner. She noticed sagging posts on Gus' side."

"Charlie, ride her horse back to the house, unsaddle her, and saddle up Mr. Jinx and Shaggy. I'm gonna follow. Meet you there."

Charlie cut across the southeast pasture and saw the dust from the dirt road under the ranch vehicle tires flying.

He beat his dad there by fifteen minutes, had Spunky unsaddled and in her stall, bridled his dad's ride, Shaggy, and had just plopped the saddle blanket and saddle on the gelding when he heard the jeep tearing up the gravel of the drive next to the house.

Out of breath, Paul ran up and assisted Charlie with saddling Mr. Jinx.

"You know where she was talking about, so you lead," Paul said, leading Shaggy out and letting Charlie go first so he could close the barn doors.

After unchaining the fence, they both went through. Charlie re-hooked the chain, and they took off at a fast gallop toward where he knew Libby had headed.

The only thing that slowed them was going through paddock fencing and closing them to secure them shut.

They arrived at the back south pasture in under twenty minutes. Father and son were thankful there were no cows nearby to spook their galloping, snorting horses.

Charlie walked Mr. Jinx toward the fence line of Lewison's property, a frown creasing his face.

"Dad, somebody's been digging here. See that?"

He pointed and got off his mount, holding the reins. His eyes scanned the ground.

Paul nudged his steed's flanks and moved forward, eyes on the ground.

"Charlie, hoof prints."

"Do they have Lib's mark?"

Paul dismounted and crouched to get a better look.

Each of the Kollers' horses had a special mark carved into the right front horseshoe. It wasn't branding—just for fun.

Libby's was a double heart, chosen when she was eight.

Paul saw a faint impression.

"Yeah, son, she was here."

He stood and followed the path of hoof marks.

"No impression of her boots, though. She didn't climb off here," he paused, "but there are footprints. There and over there."

His eyes moved over the area until he saw the brick and walked toward it.

"What in the hell is a brick doing out here?"

He didn't pick it up—worry gnawing at his heart.

"And what was someone burying?"

Charlie's gut tightened, nausea rising. Just as he was about to climb the fence, his dad stopped him.

"Son, wait. We need to get back to the house and call Chief Grayson. We don't want to be accused of trespassing and cause a legal battle. Maybe Libby's mare bucked her off and they have her but haven't called yet. Your mom's in Junction, so she wouldn't have been home to get the call."

Charlie clenched his jaw.

He wanted to storm the gates, but his father was right.

They needed to do this properly. Still, deep down, he doubted the Lewisons were helping his sister.

His fear was raw—if they didn't get to Libby, she might be lost to them forever.

***

"At lunch? Tiff, please, can't you find him? It's important. Libby's well—we can't find her, and we found her horse two miles from where we think she was." Paul Koller's voice cracked over the phone.

"Mr. Koller, I can radio him and have him call right away. Stay by the phone, okay?"

"Yeah, Tiff. Thanks." Paul disconnected.

"Dad, let's drive over there. Just ask and see if she's there?" Charlie paced a hole through the den carpet.

Paul thumped his fingers on the table.

"Okay. You take the jeep, drive over there, see if Grist is there. Maybe he was doing fence work, because that Lewison guy is not the type to dirty his hands. If you feel unsafe, leave and wait for Toby and me. Got me?"

"Yes, sir. I'll be careful."

Charlie's heart raced.

Did his dad know something about the Lewisons he hadn't shared?

If anyone hurt his sister, they were going to pay.

***

After the chief was radioed, he contacted his deputy, Chad Yarrow, to meet him at the station—fast.

"You suppose that Art fella will ask for a warrant to search his house, just to be pissy?" Chad asked.

Toby shook his head. "Yeah, he will. And we can't go trespassing either."

Chad's eyes widened. "Wow, Toby, are those some new words I ain't ever heard before?"

Toby let out a small laugh, despite the stress.

"Come on, let's get over to the Koller's. If we don't, they might take matters into their own hands—and that won't be good for anyone."

It took forty-six minutes to get to the Koller's ranch house. By then, Lindy had returned from Junction, a blubbering mess.

"Toby, you need to find my daughter. Too many kids have vanished. I can't bear the thought of..." Her voice broke as she buried her face on her husband's shoulder.

"Where's Charlie?" Deputy Yarrow asked, looking around the room.

Paul cleared his throat, his voice cracking.

"He drove over to the Lewison place to look for Harry Grist."

A deep, aggravated sigh left Chief Toby Grayson.

"Come on, Chad, let's ride over there. Can't have Charlie stepping in a pile of cow manure and getting in trouble."

36

To minimize the risk of being detected, Charlie parked his jeep at the end of the long driveway. He spotted Harry's old, battered truck near the house.

His heart pounded.

What if they had guns drawn?

What if...?

The what-ifs were consuming his rational thoughts.

This wasn't an old west movie.

Not a real-life thriller he was playing a part in.

These people weren't monsters or vampires.

He'd met them, talked to them often.

They were ordinary.

Mr. Grist he'd known for years.

Reclusive, like Gus Adair, but never scary.

His sister was gone.

Missing.

A door-to-door search was reasonable.

That was exactly what he would say.

———

Still in her dressing gown, Camille Lewison opened the door.

"May I help you?"

"Yes, ma'am. I'm Charlie. Charles Koller, your neighbor from about eight miles down the road."

"Yes, I recognize you. You're a lot older and taller." She huffed. "Now, what is it you're selling?"

Charlie's face darkened. His blue eyes sparked with anger. He was twenty, almost twenty-one. Not a kid. Not a schoolboy.

"My sister fell from her horse, and we cannot find her. The animal came back without her. She was riding fences in the south back pasture near the land that connects us and Mr. Adair at the southwest corner. I wanted to know if your man, Mr. Grist, might have seen her."

Her face twisted in disgust as she pulled at her dressing gown front.

"Well, I wouldn't know. I just came downstairs and haven't seen the hired man. I mean, he does not have the run of the house."

"Is your husband available?"

Charlie tried hard to control his anger at her persnickety attitude.

His sister might be hurt—or worse.

Someone sounded behind her.

"Camille, who is at the door?"

Art Lewison appeared, peeking around his wife, who blocked the doorway.

"Ah, Charlie, is it?"

He stuck his hand out to the boy.

Charlie shook it being polite despite himself.

When he withdrew it, he noticed three things: dirt under his fingernails, a few scratches—and blood.

"I was just explaining to the boy I slept late. Mr. Grist does not have the run of our house. The boy says he needs to speak to him. Is he working on property today?"

"I saw his truck—" Charlie began, but Art cut him off.

"I'll go find the man. Why don't you wait in the front room? Camille, let's go to the kitchen. You can fix coffee."

Without another word, he turned his wife and ushered her away, her mouth gaping at his treatment.

Charlie watched them disappear, his heart hammering.

Brotherly intuition screamed: Libby was here. In this house.

LIKE THEIR RANCH, THE house was two stories, but bigger, with more rooms.

Uncertain of Mr. Lewison's return with Grist, Charlie gambled. He ventured down the hallway next to the sitting room.

Ears on high alert, he stepped as softly as he could.

At the hall's end, he had to turn.

Left went toward the front. He went right, deeper into the house.

He reached the back near the mudroom.

A basement door loomed.

Dirt tracked the floor.

Fresh mud.

How much trouble would he be in if he went down and found nothing?

His heartbeat pounded in his ears.

Heavy steps approached.

The back door slammed.

"BOY, WHAT ARE YOU doing back here?" Art Lewison confronted him.

"Oh, crud. I was looking for the restroom. I, uh... got turned around, I suppose." Charlie's best on-the-spot answer. Perfect.

"Where is the bathroom, sir? May I borrow it?" He laughed in an unruly way. "I promise to bring it back when I'm done."

A stupid joke, but it offset the tension.

"You kids and the dumb jokes," Art pinched out through tight lips. "The restroom is down the other hall. Be quick. We'll have to go find Mr. Grist together." Lewison turned, traipsed down the hall, and disappeared around the corner.

IN THE BASEMENT, LIBBY heard her brother's voice. Heard his laugh.

Charlie had come for her.

A tear fell.

She had to give him a clue.

One foot chained.

Hands bound behind her.

Only one leg free—but by George, she wasn't letting that stop her.

Her eyes fell on a half shelf.

A box marked fragile on top.

Glass.

If her foot could reach, maybe she could push it over.

Maybe he'd hear the crash.

Libby stretched.

The tip of her boot nearly touched the box.

She drew her leg back. Fingers crossed—using the heel of her chained foot, she pushed—hard—with all her strength.

The boot flew.

The box toppled, and the sound of shattering glass echoed.

Charlie heard the crash—Lewison did, too.

The man hustled into the hall.

Charlie's hand on the door-latch.

"Got something down there, sir?"

"Got a raccoon issue. One must have set off a trap. I think you need to leave." The old man's nostrils flared.

Charlie knew he had to get help.

Raccoons or possums—or his sister.

Alive.

Breathing.

Not under a gray pile of bones.

He shuddered at the thought.

37

"YOU STAY HERE, LINDY, in case she calls," Paul said, his voice tight. "Then call Lyssa, see if she's working, ask her to come over to the house and sit with you."

Lindy blew her nose, stuck the used-up Kleenex in her pocket, and reached for the phone; she nodded.

"Paul," she looked up as she listened to the trill of a ring in her ear.

"Soon as you know something," she broke her sentence to say, "Hello, Lyssa, I need for you to come over," Lindy broke into fresh sobs.

In between her tears, she told Lyssa what was happening. Paul kissed the top of his wife's head and darted out the door to meet Toby and Deputy Yarrow.

"Paul," Toby said, "I radioed Tiff at the office, asked her to call everyone in the area, see if they've seen your girl, and to report back. You follow me in your truck, and we'll go to the Lewison's, 'cause that's where you sent Charlie, ain't it?"

A frown stiffened on Paul's face. "You would have too, Toby. Don't say you wouldn't. I told Charlie to sit and watch, but if my boy went in and is in danger too, then we best be hauling our asses, don'tcha think?"

Toby needed to get there first, because guns or no guns, or any lack of weapons wouldn't keep Paul Koller from doing serious harm to anyone who threatened his children.

———

THE STANDOFF BETWEEN ART and Charlie at the closed door of the basement ended when Harry Grist walked in.
"Mr. Lewison, you needed me?"
"Have you seen this boy's sister today?"
Harry's forehead wrinkled.
"No, haven't seen nobody except you folks."
Before Charlie could ask Mr. Grist if he'd been in the south pasture, Art said, "Later I need for you to go down in the basement. I think we've trapped a raccoon, but right now can you get the Lincoln out of the garage and pull it up front?"
"Yes, sir," Grist said, and left.
"Let me show you to the door, son."
Art placed a hand on Charlie's shoulder, and he shrugged it off.
"I'm not your son. Your son is gone, or did you forget that?"
His words spat in anger, as he stepped back.
"Boy, you are on thin ice here, and if you don't leave I am going to contact the police."
Charlie stood to his full height—five foot eleven—and puffed out his chest.
"Go ahead, because my dad already called them and they're on their way out here."

BELOW, IN THE BASEMENT, Libby rubbed her shoulder against the corner of her mouth, trying to roll the duct tape off.

She stretched her lips and relaxed them—repeated the motion as the tape lifted from her bottom lip.

Using her tongue, she pushed at the sticky side, caught it on her top teeth, and bit down, pulling it inward.

Her breathing labored with the hysterical panic to get it off so she could scream.

Charlie glared at the man.

A sudden shift occurred in Mr. Lewison's attitude.

His once helpful demeanor transitioned into inflexible anger.

Change was apparent in his hard eyes and clipped speech.

"Get out of my house. Now."

"I'm not going far, sir, just to the edge of your property line to wait for Chief Grayson and my father. I will be back."

He turned to leave and just as he'd taken one step—he heard her.

"CHARLIE! Help me, help me!"

And the scream that followed was ear-piercing.

His elbow came back, catching the old man in the gut, sending him to his knees, and Charlie pushed past him, his hand on the latch of the cellar door.

Art grabbed his foot, and Charlie stumbled, but was able to get his ankle out of the old guy's grasp with a kick backwards.

In the kitchen, Camille heard the commotion.

Her voice raised. "What on earth is going on?"

Her dressing gown snagged her foot as she ran, resulting in a face-plant on the floor.

She hit her elbow on the corner of the doorway and shrieked in pain.

Art heard Camille but didn't care. He was still trying to keep Charlie out of the basement.

Then he had another thought.

Why not shove him in, then lock the door?

Only the kid said the police and his dad were on the way.

He didn't have the time to tie him up and re-tape the girl's mouth.

Only what if?

If the boy was shoved hard enough, he'd either, one, break his neck, or two, get knocked out.

Art's thoughts jumped again to, "oh my god, what will I do with two more bodies?"

It was over, and he knew it.

Life had just ended for one Arthur David Lewison. He let go of Charlie's arm, straightened his shirt, and went to find Camille, who was on the floor, writhing, holding her right arm in pain.

After he'd helped her up and to the sitting room, he went for a dishcloth and filled it with ice.

Charlie flung open the door to the cellar and raced down the steps to find his baby sister; feeling so relieved he wrapped his arms around her, hugging and crying.

Libby sobbed, her words said in huffs between her crying: "Oh, Charlie Brown, you came for me, you did, oh, thank you, you came, you came."

He leaned back and wiped his eyes. He peeled the last stubborn strips of tape from her cheek and hair, then drew his hunting knife and snipped the zip ties binding her hands—eyeing the chain and lock like a puzzle yet to be solved.

"The key? Libby, did you see where he put it?"
Libby's head gestured toward the wall near the last
step as she rubbed her wrists.
"On that hook."
In no time flat, Charlie had her unchained and up.
He examined her head and was thankful it wasn't a
large gash.
"Libby, did he, are you, hurt anywhere else?"
He hadn't seen torn clothing, and he prayed very hard
for her answer not to have him seeing red.
"No, he only locked me up down here. He didn't do,
uh, that," Libby shuddered. "Can we get outta here,
please?"
With his arm around her shoulder, Charlie guided
her up the steps, ready to defend her—and him-
self—against anyone who dared to bother them.
When they reached the last step, he heard the pound-
ing on the door, and the voice of his father.
"My jeep's out here, so where is my son, and he'd
better not be hurt."
"Paul, settle, let me handle this," Grayson said, then:
"Mrs. Lewison, are you hurt?"
At the top of the cellar stairs, Charlie looked at Libby
and shrugged. He had no idea what had happened to
the woman.
"My wife might have a fractured arm, not sure. We
need to get her to the hospital in Junction," Art said.
Two faces appeared around the corner and into the
room, and Paul Koller rushed to his children.
"Charlie, Libby, oh my lord, are you okay?"
With a rush of relief, he embraced them, the frantic
pace of his racing heart slowing to a steady beat as he
held them close.
"Kids, my babies," his words brushed against their

heads as he kissed each of them.

"Deputy Yarrow," Toby started, but stopped when another person walked into the room.

Harry Grist.

"The Lincoln is..." Grist stopped when he saw the chief of police, his deputy, Koller and his two children; Camille sat holding her arm moaning, and Art Lewison.

A deep pent-up sigh left the hired man's chest.

It was over.

He would be questioned, and if so, he was going to ask for a lawyer first—a deal second.

The police chief told Harry to take a seat, then instructed his deputy to call the volunteer fire department and have them send their EMTs over since that was faster. "Radio Tiff, have her call the sheriff's office and ask them to meet us in town."

Toby looked at Libby. "Do you need medical care, sweetheart?"

She shook her head. "No, sir, I don't think so. He, uh, didn't, well he didn't. Only the blasted brick caught me in the temple; it just sheared me because I tried to dodge it, only I hit hard when I got tossed off my horse..." she paused, "Spunky, where's my mare?"

Libby's eyes sparked hate. If her horse was harmed, she'd kill that man.

"Baby," Paul calmed her, "we found Spunk. She's in her stall and safe."

Those words relaxed the young girl, and she sank into her father's side and gave Art a look of pure loathing.

"Okay, then. Paul, you drive your kids to town, meet us. And, uh, Mr. Grist?"

Toby turned his attention to the hired man. "I want you to ride into town with the Kollers, you got it?"

Harry removed his dirty old John Deere hat, held it in both hands in front of him, and nodded. "Yes, sir, I will."

Toby thought for a second, then said, "And I'd rather the four of you not talk about anything on the ride to town. Is that clear?"

Paul, Charlie, Libby, and Grist all nodded their understanding.

"EMTs be here in ten, Chief," Yarrow said.

"Chad, radio Tiff, ask her to call Lindy Koller. Tell her we have her daughter. She's safe, and so are her son and husband."

He looked at Paul. "Phone her from the station when you get there."

He turned his attention to the couple on the sofa. "Mr. Lewison, you need to stand up and turn around."

The man did, and he aged twenty years before everyone's eyes.

"Arthur Lewison, you are under arrest for kidnapping Libby Koller. You have the right to remain silent—"

Toby cuffed and finished, then asked him if he understood his rights.

A sullen Art nodded; a shocked Camille's mouth opened, then closed as she frowned up at her spouse. Flabbergasted and unaware of what had transpired, she asked him, "Art, did you kidnap that girl?" Her eyes slid over to Libby.

"Camille, my dear, you haven't heard the worst of it." A smug smile stretched across his face.

38

THE STORY BROKE, AND it was the biggest news to hit this area—ever.

Hotspur was now on the map.

Only, this tragic tale was not how the residents of the small, yet growing, community had wanted to make their name known.

Harry Grist had struck a deal: no jail time for the murders. Still, he was charged with corpse tampering—he'd interred the bodies of Cathy Nunez and Doug Lewison and removed Doug's skeleton a second time.

The County attorney handed the case to the District Attorney. Grist faced a hefty fine and a sentence of two years per body on a second-degree felony charge.

Art Lewison, however, was a different story.

A man with countless terrible tales, he offered everything.

If he were going to be charged and convicted of Cathy and Doug's murders, why hold back?

He wasn't a cat with nine lives, keeping seven—his life was over. So why not make a name for himself, even if it meant an infamously lived life behind cold steel bars?

He confessed to Wanda Elaine Roberts from Dorchester in 1955; Frannie Swisher in 1986; Cathy Nunez and Doug Lewison in 1987.

He regaled officials with tales of his nephew-slash-adoptive son, Douglas Gordon Lewison, his cruelty to a kitten, the runaway Marlin Hudson, and suspicions about Doug's involvement in the death of Missy Van der Bern.

Camille was horrified at Art's revelations, but she broke down, turning over papers and photos she had hidden in their wall safe.

Those documents, and Doug's own journal, proved yet another murder her son had committed at just fourteen, alongside terrors inflicted on neighbors' pets.

The bones were recovered.

Cathy Nunez and Doug Lewison were identified.

Her remains were sent to her family in Wickett, Texas, for a proper burial, though, sadly, her father had passed. Her remaining family had tried to forget and had not wanted her remains, so Hotspur's townspeople buried her skeletal remnants in the local cemetery at their expense, marked only with a metal cross.

The Swisher family received confirmation: the girl's abductor and killer had been apprehended. Painful memories resurfaced—yes—but there was closure.

Doug's remains were sent to Boston, laid to rest with his parents.

Camille stayed on until Art's trial concluded. For her, there was a morbid satisfaction in watching the man she'd once thought loved her drown in the sea of his own damnation.

It came out in full: he married her for money, hated her, hated Doug, hated it all.

The judge's gavel fell.

Art Lewison was found guilty on multiple charges.

A wicked, satisfied smile crept across Camille's face.

Had Art ever loved Doug—or her—perhaps things would have been different. She would not have lost the one thing she truly loved: her son.

Art Lewison was charged with four counts of murder, two counts of kidnapping (Libby and the Swisher girl), unlawful burial of a corpse, and every other charge the DA could throw at him. Even then, no one in Hotspur thought it enough.

***

"Sensationalized news and the press—I feel smothered," Libby groaned as they left the courthouse.

"It will die down. Be forgotten," her mother said, patting her hand.

"Not if they keep dogging us about writing our story," Libby said, resting her head against her mother's shoulder in the back seat of the old Suburban.

"Hey, Libby, I got an idea." Gregg was back in town for the ordeal—the only silver lining for Libby. She'd missed her big brother, who was in the final year of his internship in Waco, Texas.

"What's that, Greggy?"

"Write your story. Sell a million copies. Buy Mom a new Suburban. Big Red here is on her last leg."

"No way, big brother. I think I'll pass. Sorry, Mom." Libby smiled.

"I'll drive Big Red till the wheels fall off. Besides, I was gonna bequeath her to you, Gregg. You'll need a vehicle to haul sick animals. This baby is big!"

Paul and Charlie laughed.

———

CAMILLE STOOD OUTSIDE THE house.

A Mayflower Moving truck had just turned out of the drive, her cousin from Boston and his wife waiting in a rented car.

Family she had few of—and she needed them.

They had agreed to help.

An estate planner had helped downsize.

Everything she owned that was sellable was gone. Even parts of the house. It was stripped of personality, and charm—not that it had ever mattered.

Sal Grayson called off the surveyors and lifted the injunction determining property lines. After law enforcement cleared the crime scene, the land sale went through.

By midnight, the developers held full claim.

In a blink, subdivisions would rise. Blacktop roads, mail stations, brick walls, wrought iron fencing, schools at the center of larger communities. Pools, basketball courts, ponds—off-limits to boating, swimming, or fishing. What was fun about that? Country kids would wonder.

Grocery stores would multiply to feed families.

Shops to clothe and entertain them.

Progress would sweep through Hotspur, Dove Crossing, River Run—and even Link—overnight.

Elementary schools, junior highs, senior highs.

Technology expanding horizons.

Times were changing.

The old dying.

The young growing.

Nothing would stop it.
Land was there—but being covered by the acre.
Only a few would hold fast, their land embedded in
hearts and souls.
They'd keep it and never sell out.

Epilogue

1994

Six months after the ordeal, Paul and Charlie pulled up to the farmhouse and waved at Gus, who sat on his front porch snapping green beans from his garden. He waved back.

"Drag ya up a chair. You fellers want some sweet tea?" The old guy set his metal bowl down, wiped his hands, and shook first Paul's, then Charlie's hands.

"Not me, but thanks," said Charlie. His father echoed the same.

"You two checking up on this old man, huh?"

They weren't fooling anyone, so they both shrugged, and Paul said, "Yeah, guess we are, since all this mess started."

"After all this court stuff was over and no more digging for bones on or near my property, I feel I got my life back. Terrible business and glad they got that killer behind bars. Heard he was gonna get death row, too."

The three sat there contemplating that thought. No one wanted to be a death judge and say he got what he deserved—at least not out loud.

"Say, Charlie," Gus glanced over, "you got some time on your hands in a few days?"

"Yes, sir. Whatcha need?"

"Got some goats I wanna take to the Auction House at the end of the week. Wanna see if you and Bruce might ride with me."

"Bruce left for Kansas last week. He took a job on an old rig and won't be back for a few months. How about I get Libby to go with us instead?"

"That sister of yours, she sure is a pip."

Paul Koller chimed in, "She is gonna make some rancher fella an excellent wife, if she ever gets to dating."

They chatted for a spell, helping Gus snap a few bowls of green beans before Paul stood. "We should probably go home. The cows need feeding, and your mom's gonna be worried."

Gus set his bowl aside. "You two wait a minute."

He went into the house and, in a few minutes, came back out with an empty Cheerios box stuffed with fresh poke salad and an empty lunch sack, then filled it with fresh garden green beans.

"Give this to Lindy. Got too much for just me."

He grinned, showing his tobacco-stained teeth, then sat back down in his metal rocker and pulled the half-filled bowl into his lap, reaching for another handful of unsnapped green beans.

Paul and Charlie walked to the truck with their fresh vegetables, and Gus called out, "Thank you, guys. Can't ask for no better neighbors than you."

Charlie turned, waved, and smiled. Paul called out, "Any time, Gus. You need us, just call."

THEY DROVE IN SILENCE. The ride down the gravel road to the main road was bumpy, and Paul turned onto the older two-lane blacktop three miles later.

"Dad?"

"Yeah?"

"We're supposed to get mom some stuff from the store. You forget?"

"Shoot! Let's turn around and go to Gilmores. Hotspur's closer than Junction."

"Dad, go to the Piggly Wiggly, goober."

"Dang, Charlie, old habits die hard with your old man. I keep forgetting we got that store since I don't do the food shopping."

"I know, Dad. Times are changing, huh?"

Paul Koller nodded. "Yep, son, they are at that. Listen, about the ranch..."

"No, Dad, I haven't changed my mind. It's what I want to do. I don't want you and Mom to sell it. I can run it, after—well, you know what I mean."

"Son, will you at least think about a two-year college? Go to Angelo State and get a business degree?"

"I promise to think about it, Dad, but that's it, okay?"

"All I can ask for, son."

Paul slowed the truck and pulled over onto the gravel shoulder.

"Why are we stopping, Dad?"

"Come on, get out."

The boy's eyebrows furrowed, but he climbed out and trudged toward the truck bed, where his dad was standing.

"Look out there, Charlie. What do you see?"

He squinted, looking for a deer, a coyote, even a wild hog—nothing. Just land.

"Nothing's there, Pop." His brows dipped, not knowing what his dad meant for him to see.

Paul put his arm around his son's shoulders. "Charlie boy, it was about ten years ago, and you told me something, and in such a poetic way, you sorta told the future."

"I did?" Charlie side-glanced at his father.

Paul lifted his hand and pointed to the back of the land. "See those heaps of brush?"

Charlie followed his dad's fingers, his eyes landing on the three piles of dead brush in the distance.

A sharp gasp escaped him. "Yeah, Dad, I remember. I said... those look like a pile of gray bones."

"Yep, you did. And I said they look like what they are. Only, maybe, son, you knew something we all didn't."

Charlie narrowed his eyes. A pile of gray bones. Yes, they'd found two bodies under a heap like that, and the odds were astronomical that would happen in this small town.

"Well, Pop. I think it meant more than the two kids. I think those heaps tell us that life is changing along with the landscape."

"Charlie boy, I think you hit the nail on the head with that. I sure do."

The End

Acknowledgements

Again thank you to my Beta readers- Sharon Jaeger and Ed Kearns; taking time to read my work and giving me your thoughts is more than appreciated. To my Husband, Travis. Thanks for your continued support and for listening to me read EVERYDAY while you drove home.

Author's Note

Word-of-mouth is crucial for any author to succeed. If you enjoyed A Pile of Gray Bones, please leave a review online—anywhere you are able. Even if it's just a sentence or two; it would make all the difference and would be very much appreciated.

Thanks,
Deanna

Scan ME!

Deannakingwriting.com

About the Author

A Pile of Gray Bones is Deanna King's first YA suspense Novel. Ms. King lives with her husband Travis and two very spoiled dogs in Texas.

www.ingramcontent.com/pod-product-compliance
Lightning Source LLC
Chambersburg PA
CBHW011342010726
47493CB00009B/2917